Highwayman
War's End

MICHAEL ARNOLD

First published 2020 by Sharpe Books.

For my niece, Isla

Table of Contents

JANUARY 1656

Grange Farm, Petersfield, Hampshire

A vixen's cry shredded the night.

Startled, the thief crouched low against the crumbling cob wall, the rasp of his heaving chest overlaid by the rushing blood at his ears. The surviving three fingers of his right hand were braced against his thigh and he dug the nails hard through the wool of his breeches, relaxing his grip only when the pain had chased away the panic. He swore softly at his own temerity, reminding himself of the growl in his belly and edged eyes and nose above the makeshift parapet.

The pirates were directly to the south, forty paces away or thereabouts. He counted them in silence. Eleven, all present and correct, seated on logs and discarded barrels, knees drawn up before the remnants of a glowing fire. The men were at the centre of an unpaved yard, its craggy terrain of wheel-ruts and boot-prints frozen solid by the bitter winter. Beyond them, looming over the farm's half-dozen outbuildings, was the great barn, its stone walls pale in the moonlight, soaring rooftop gilded by a gossamer of frost. Distant storm clouds swelled and rolled far beyond, surging in from the coast.

Outside the barn, its shafts roped to iron rings set into the building's masonry, was the high-sided wagon the pirates had brought with them. The thief had watched as their weapons and personal effects were stowed within. Absently, he wondered why they did not seek shelter inside the barn.

The pirates laughed and chatted. One of them took a long drag from an earthenware flask and spat into the orange embers, causing a tell-tale hiss and a flare of new flame. A man struck up a slow tune on a flageolet, another of his comrades accompanying him with a mournful voice. The thief waited and watched. He checked over his shoulder, squinting through the darkness to perceive the outline of the town, chimney stacks silhouetted by the moon, thin smoke-trails smearing the stars. Locating the line of the Portsmouth road, he let his eyes trace its route towards the farm, dipping low before rising again as it passed him, becoming the long, straight causeway that elevated travellers above the treacherous, marshy terrain on their way into the chalky hills. All was empty, all was silent. He pulled on his trusty Montero cap, tugging the sides down to cup his face and slung his snapsack over a shoulder.

To the thief's right, at the west of the yard, a flurry of sound came from a low timber block as the pirates' pair of bulky brown draught horses bickered with their new stablemates in the stalls. One of the men around the fire snarled a command. No-one bothered to investigate but their attention had been collectively engaged and they all squinted towards the stable in the gloom. The thief thanked God for His providence, pressed closer to the wall and prayed hard.

The prayer was answered more swiftly than he could have hoped. Soft whickering grew to a chorus of angry whinnies as the cramped horses jostled for space and fodder, all of it played out above the beat of iron-shod hooves against the stable walls. This time the thief did not wait to see if the men reacted. He was already on the move. He vaulted the wall, ignoring the scrape of loose stones and scuttled, hunched and crablike, into the open. His breath was white in the biting air, haloing his wool-wrapped skull, a beacon for his every movement. He clamped shut his mouth, allowed himself only to pant through his nostrils in sharp, shallow bursts and prayed that he might be spared the watchman's cry.

Gradually the horses became calm but still the pirate sang his melancholy refrain. And the thief went to work.

TUESDAY

Idsworth, Hampshire

St Peter's Church stood alone on a high sweep of chalk downland as the storm vented its fury. Stinging rain beat at the valley in diagonal sheets, dashing the isolated building's flint walls and forming rivulets between the roof tiles that bubbled and gushed as they poured onto the gravel path below. The surrounding hills seemed to quiver as their deeply forested slopes leaned before winds that screamed like a host of banshees, the last vestiges of snow purged ruthlessly from the highest boughs. Above the straining canopy, boisterous rooks banked and twirled beneath bruise-coloured skies. Through it all, a single bell began to peel, its mournful call echoing stubbornly from crest to crest.

On the chalk ridge, the doors of the little church groaned open. Figures swathed in heavy winter coats and cassocks, streamed in pairs from the west porch, some linking arms against the howling gale, all tilting forwards as if wading through treacle. The procession fought its way along a track that cut through a wide field, sloping down towards the main road some two hundred paces below. There they would find the waiting carriages, drawn up in a long line before the gated entrance to a substantial, if a touch dogeared, manor house. Coachmen squinted back up the rise, shielding rain-slick faces with wide hats and waxed sleeves, attempting to locate their masters as swiftly as possible so that they might flee the hostile afternoon. Irritable horses whinnied and snorted. The road's edge, still patched with thawing slush, steamed and turned yellow beneath their raised tails.

From the porch, the elderly man placed a woollen cap upon

his snow-white pate and watched the last of the storm-harried congregation fight their way to the roadside, hands clamped tight to their own hats, wasting no time on pleasantries as they clambered into their vehicles. He saw the carriages lurch, heard the whips crack above the whining wind. Drivers barked, their voices deep and resonant below the shrill caws of the obdurate rooks. The old man could not stifle a rueful smile. The great and the good of the parish would walk into the very eye of a hurricane if there were enough witnesses to report it. As dusk crept ever closer, he felt sure word of their attendance on this most inclement day would spread like the sickness that had placed his beloved wife in the very casket around which they had all brandished their piety. Some, he knew, had come here out of genuine grief. Most had come to be seen.

The old man made to turn. It was then that he glimpsed the rider.

The horse was huge and grey, a pale smudge emerging from a stand of bare trees at the northern fringe of the ridge. In the saddle, hunched against the rain, was a figure draped in a cloak of dark green. A man, to judge by a frame that looked tall and lean but broad at the shoulders. Water dripped from the hem of his deep hood and from his long scabbard's pointed chape. They loped, man and beast, across the downland swell, buffeted on both sides by the malicious wind, the horse's fetlocks caked in mud. They were heading for the church.

The old man went inside. The nave echoed with the sound of his own footsteps. He searched the plain benches, the whitewashed walls, the little pulpit. He was alone. The bell continued to toll. He turned in the direction of the bell turret. There was, at least, one person left. A creak at his back. It was too late. He fished for the chinking purse at his belt, fumbling with the string so that it might be hidden.

"Master Spendlove."

The old man looked up at the speaker, the purse still clutched tight in his trembling hand. "I have, this afternoon, put my wife in the ground, sirrah. Have you no respect?"

The newcomer, standing in a gathering pool of rainwater, drew back his hood and glanced around the church. "She loved it here."

Spendlove gaped. "You." His mouth dried. He made a show of looking over his shoulder. "The rector is within."

The man in the green cloak gave a sardonic smile. "Busy at his chimes." He spread gloved hands wide. "I mean you no ill, Master. How long has it been since last we spoke? A decade? I am sorry for that, yet still I grieve with you. Does that offend?"

Spendlove groped for words that were suddenly elusive, managing only a murmured, "No." He let his gaze roam over the tall man's features. Over eyes that were green like the cloak but paler, cooler and unsettlingly keen. They sat above a prominent nose that bore the kink of a long-healed break and a cleanly-shaven chin that was strong in an otherwise spare, thin-lipped face. The man's hair was a tousled mop, the colour of straw and his complexion was lined and weathered, though Spendlove knew the cragginess to be premature; owing to matters beyond the mere passage of time. He swallowed thickly, finding his voice. "You knew her. To mourn her is your right, just as it is mine."

The tall man winced as he bowed. "I loved her." He shifted his stance, suddenly awkward, the tall riding boots – bucket-tops pulled high over his thighs – clacking on the flagstones.

"You called her aunt."

"She was a second mother. When I heard of her passing, I knew it was to this old place that I should come."

A memory crept unbidden into Spendlove's mind and he could not help but smile. "You ever chided us, Ursula and I, for coming here."

The tall man grinned. "Chalton is your village, Master. Furnished with its own place of worship." The pale eyes surveyed the modest church again. There was the hint of a shudder. "Idsworth is a haunt of ghosts."

Spendlove pushed a lock of hair back under the edge of his cap. "But this ancient place lingers, in spite of it all. A symbol of the life that once thrived on these hills."

"A place now only of sorrow."

"Of stillness and contemplation." As he spoke, Spendlove noticed the hilt of the rider's sword, protruding through the cloak at his waist. It had an elaborate shell guard, the metal decorated with holes cut into the shapes of stars and hearts. It was a famous sword. No, an *infamous* sword. The sight of it jogged his mind, permitting the return of gnawing disquiet. "You should not be here."

The lean face tightened. "I will leave if that pleases."

Spendlove almost laughed at that. "Nothing of what has become of you pleases me, boy." The alternating waves of astonishment and anxiety gave way now to anger. He pressed a hand to his chest as he spoke in a cracking voice. "It is a dagger to my heart, Samson, as it was to hers."

"I did not wish to dismay you, Master," the rider blurted, the confidence fading from his tone. He reached out a hand, failing to conceal another wince. "That was not my intention."

"Dismay me?" Spendlove shrugged him off, twisting to one of the wooden benches, at the end of which was a short stack of pamphlets. He snatched one up, wielding it before the rider like a weapon. "You dismayed me, Samson Lyle, when you became the Ironside Highwayman."

Samson Lyle had been advised not to come. Had been subjected to a spittle-flecked rant during which the risks of coming out into the open had been colourfully extolled. He had ignored every word. Laughed the worries away. But now, as he paced at Spendlove's side, the bell's continuing toll reverberating about the high roof beams, he began to wonder at his own hubris. He glanced down at the man who had taught him to read and write, who had breathed life into Classical Greece and the emperors of Rome, who had introduced the joy of Shakespeare, Marlow and Johnson. A man to whom Lyle owed so much, yet whose disappointment hurt more than any sword thrust. He said meekly, "I had no choice."

They were walking down the nave, towards the porch. Spendlove did not look up. "There is always a choice, Samson."

Skirting a magnificent octagonal font decorated with quatrefoiled panels, Lyle noticed its broad base bore the marks of recent repair. He recalled hearing how the ancient object had been smashed by Parliament men during the war. Nothing but nothing, had been left unsullied by those bitter years, he thought. "You know what they did to her?" he asked tightly, feeling bile rise at the mere thought.

The porch, as they stepped inside, was still shut but the wind howled like a pack of wolves beyond the studded door. Spendlove turned to him now. His face was lined like an ancient map but his blue eyes were as bright as Lyle remembered. "Of course. And I grieve with you, Samson, as you grieve with me but that does not give you the right to..."

Lyle had reached for the door's large iron ring. He let it go. "But do you know what happened?"

Spendlove's white eyebrows knitted together. "Kicked by a horse. A tragedy, Samson. God called your goodwife home, just as He has mine." He raised an admonishing finger, the school master resurrected. "That is no justification for what you have become."

"God did not call," Lyle said scornfully, his mind making the inexorable leap to another time and place, delving deep to mine seams of perfect sorrow. "Alice was dispatched." He had hissed the final word and regretted the rancour in his voice but was powerless to dilute it. "Thrust through the veil beneath the hooves of my enemies. Murdered out of spite that was meant for me."

The old man recoiled as though taking a dagger to the chest. "Murdered?"

"Trampled," Lyle said, voice clotting. He had not been present on that fateful day. En route, instead, to France and four years of exile. But still he relived Alice's killing every time he closed his eyes. Replayed every shout, every command, every scream. "They killed her because I was not there to kill. I am outside the law, Master and I know how it must unsettle you but the Army is *above* the law. Lambert and Cromwell and the rest." He heard himself laugh, though it was a dark, mirthless sound. "Major-General Goffe is ruler of Berkshire, Sussex and Hampshire. He *makes* the law. Bends it to his will. Who will resist, if not I?"

"Is that what Alice would have wanted? For you to forfeit your own life in her absence?"

"Alice is no longer in a position to want anything. And my life saw ruination the day I lost her. Thus, I shall haunt these roads. I shall hunt the Major-General's men. I will harry their convoys and I will make their lives unbearable, as they have made mine unbearable."

The silence that filled the porch was like a noxious fog, stifling them both. Lyle drew up his hood and went back to the door.

Spendlove reached for his elbow. "You mourn Ursula with me. I mourn Alice with you. Let us leave it at that. I harbour no ill-will, Samson. God knows there are plenty who do but I do not."

Lyle felt a torrent of relief. It was unexpected and for a

moment he was dumbstruck. What had he hoped for, coming here? He had told himself it was an errand simply to pay his respects. Told his criminal associates, Eustace and Bella, that such gauntlets were there to be run. Yet now that he had received some measure of acceptance from his old tutor, he realised that was all he had wanted. He stooped, gathering Spendlove in his arms and hugging him tight. "Thank you, Master."

"Still, you should not be here," Spendlove whispered. "You run a great risk."

Lyle straightened. "Soldiers? Here?"

Spendlove shook his head. "But there is not a lane or bridleway they do not patrol."

Lyle shot him a crooked smile. "Even down in these forgotten places?"

Spendlove tutted, rebuking him as he had once done so often. "You mock, Samson but I will ever cherish poor Idsworth. The black death killed the people, right enough and left it empty. Nothing to show out there but a few crumbling walls and pastureland left for the forest to devour. Now it is mere memory."

"A memory with a church."

Spendlove turned back to examine the interior, his gaze wistful. "This place has seen much. Lost much." He pointed to the whitewashed chancel arch and the walls beyond. "There are wondrous murals here, Samson. Tales of scripture rendered in vibrant colour. Concealed after the fissure with Rome. My grandfather told me of those days. Of the men who came with grim faces and full buckets and sang Psalms as they purged every sublime brushstroke from every inch of every wall. But they linger, those marvellous creations. Hidden. Waiting for their time to come again."

Lyle arched an eyebrow. "And I suppose that *I* am St Peter's church, yes?" he said wryly. "A monument to memories stifled and concealed."

Spendlove pursed his lips in an expression of innocence. "Your words, Samson. Not mine." He winked. "But the murals here will one day bask in daylight. I pray what is buried in your soul will find its own way out."

"One day."

"And until then?"

"I have made my bed and I shall lie in it." Lyle opened the door. The wind threw it wide, almost wrenching off his arm to press the point. He hissed as white-hot pain lanced his left shoulder blade.

"Samson?"

"It is nothing," Lyle said. "I was wounded, before Christmas. Pistol ball. It heals nicely."

"Jesus love you, boy," Spendlove replied, shaking his head in astonishment.

"Come." Lyle staggered out into the rain-lashed open. The gloom was gathering apace. "It grows late, Master. These roads are not safe."

"Should I fear highwaymen?"

Lyle grinned. "Footpads, I was going to say." He had to shout to be heard, gripping a fistful of his hood just to keep it up. "Plenty shelter in the high hills. I would escort you back to Chalton."

The old man indicated a lone, open-topped carriage down on the road, its single palfrey sheltering beneath a tree. "I have my trap."

"And I my horse," Lyle said. "Poor devil's tethered 'neath a tree. Charred black by lightning by now, I shouldn't wonder."

"Let us travel together, then," Spendlove demurred, resigning himself to company. "There is a small gathering at the inn. Well-wishers, you understand. You remember the Red Lion?"

Lyle laughed. "I have become an outlaw, Master Spendlove, not a half-wit."

A cinder path took them to a beech tree, alone on the grassy hillock, its crooked branches making defiant gestures at the darkening skies. Lyle led the way, dipping his head against the rain while the bell sang on.

"Chalton will be busy," Spendlove muttered at his back, rapid strides crunching in the dusk. "You'll be seen."

"I am seen a great deal," Lyle said, squinting into the tangle of low boughs under which his pale horse shifted uneasily. "Context is all. If they do not expect to see a notorious highwayman, they will not see one. Besides, those who knew my face before the wars are few and far between. And I, of course, am hardly the fresh young stripling that once they knew."

"You have not changed as much as you might think," Spendlove replied. "You're as cocksure as ever and that's a fact."

Lyle smirked into the driving rain. "I feel I have changed a great deal but perhaps I delude myself. And what of little Botolph and Amelia?"

"They will be there," Spendlove said, presumably meaning the alehouse in Chalton.

"How do they do?"

"Grown now, almost. Amelia turned eighteen, July last. A man could not wish for a better daughter, though, Jesu forgive her, in possession of a loud mouth and a hot head," he chuckled, "not so dissimilar to your own."

"Her mother was the bold one, as I recall."

"Aye," Spendlove agreed with an aching sigh, "bold and courageous was dear Ursula."

"Botolph was the younger of the two," Lyle remembered.

Spendlove nodded. “By three years. A gentle lad but a good one. I thank the Lord for them both daily.”

“I can trust them?”

“You can.”

“Then I look forward to paying my respects.”

They were ten yards out from the tree but Spendlove halted. “You intend to step foot in the tavern? This is folly, Samson and no mistake.”

“If I am recognised, I will depart,” Lyle reassured him, “after a positively Shakespearean display of blackguardly roguishness, of course. One mustn't have you implicated, after all. Perhaps I shall relieve you of a groat or two and you can play the stoic victim.”

Spendlove fiddled with his hat, worry etched on the deep fissures of his face. “It is no laughing matter, Samson and...”

A raised palm cut him off. Movement had caught Lyle's eye. He stared through the blurring rain. His horse, Star, was there, the big stallion's grey coat a pastel smear amongst the gnarled tangle of branches but something was out of kilter. Something in the beast's movement, an odd crabbing, as though Star were shying from some danger at his flank.

Lyle ran. The wind snatched back his hood. The rain streaked his face. He ducked under the first bough, skirted another and he was into the patch of bare earth around the beech, a clearing rendered flat and barren by the tree's canopy. Star was there, attached to the truck by his reins but he was not alone.

“Put your sticky paws where I might see them, friend,” Lyle ordered, lifting his voice above the rush of raindrops on leaves. He came to stand some half-dozen paces from the man who had been rifling through his saddlebags.

The man was short and wiry, clothed in rough apparel little superior than those of a beggar. His head was covered in a woollen cap, the sides unfurled to shield ears and frame a face that was pinched and rat-like. He was clearly startled but he managed to produce a short, curved knife from the snapsack slung at his shoulder. He jutted out his narrow chin and sneered. "Or what, *friend*?"

Lyle thrust a hand into the folds of his cloak and pulled the pistol from his belt. "Or you shall witness my weekly shooting practise at uncomfortably close quarters."

The man – who, to Lyle's reckoning, looked to have seen a handful more years than his own twenty-seven – let his mouth loll open, exposing the remains of blackened teeth and diseased gums. He spoke with a broad northern accent that was marked by a high-pitched whistle on the letter 's'. "What is that thing?"

The thing in question was one of Lyle's most cherished possessions. Created for a wealthy Frenchman by a Rotterdam gunsmith, it had found its way to him after a brawl in a Rennes alehouse during his time in exile. Longer than a typical English flintlock, the weapon was no less wieldy, its balance and workmanship exquisite. But what made it truly special was its ability to fire two shots in quick succession. "Double barrelled pistol," Lyle said, turning his hand a touch so that the reedy man might see it with more clarity. "Two strikers, two muzzles but the same lock, cock and flint." He trained the gun on the man's face. "One bullet for each of your eyes."

The stranger edged away from the horse but did not relinquish his blade. Around the hilt, his knuckles were white where he gripped and Lyle noticed that he was missing his two middle fingers. His eyes, gleaming brown beads beneath the edge of the brown cap, flickered restlessly between Lyle's face and the twin muzzles. "You'd kill a man in a church yard?"

"You'd rob a man in one? Besides, where better, sirrah?" Lyle jerked back his head in the general direction of St Peter's. "I believe the gravediggers are still here, as luck would have it. The ground's nice and malleable and I'd be delighted to lend them a hand."

The fidgety eyes narrowed a fraction, the thin upper lip curling. "Trust your powder to burn, do you?"

Lyle shrugged. "Do you trust that it won't?" A tightening of the northern fellow's expression spoke for his indecision and Lyle twitched the pistol. "Put the blade down, man, for Christ's sake."

Down it went, landing on its side in the leaf mulch. Down, too, fell its owner's façade. "I meant no harm, sirs," the three-fingered man blurted, his bluster leaking rapidly away while his gaze darted beyond Lyle's shoulder.

Lyle looked round to see that Spendlove had managed to pick his way beneath the beech's knotted limbs. "A would-be thief," he announced, throwing his gaze quickly over the horse to ensure nothing was missing. One holster was necessarily empty, its occupant currently in his grip but the butt of the second pistol, a regular flintlock, was present. Lower down, fastened in a leather loop, there glinted the fearsome war-hammer he had carried since the late rebellion, while his saddlebags did not appear to sag with tell-tale emptiness. He returned to his captive. "And what is the thief's name?"

"Thief, sir?" the man carped. "No no, not I."

"I suggest you return whatever trinkets you may have stolen," Lyle went on, ignoring the mealy-mouthed protest, "and tell me what business, other than the obvious, you have hereabouts." The villain, he decided, obviously required a timely reminder, so he moved the folds of his cloak aside to expose the hilt of his sword. "I am on familiar terms with Colonel Maddocks, if that serves to jolt your memory."

The words worked as surely as any dagger thrust. Foreboding etched itself into the northerner's sharp features. "The commander hereabouts?"

"You have heard of him, then?"

"Aye, sir. Who has not?"

"An old acquaintance of mine," Lyle said, which, in the most basic of terms, was true enough. It rankled to invoke the name of his nemesis and he heard Spendlove shift his feet. He turned to shoot him a wry glance. "Needs must when the devil drives, Master."

Spendlove held his peace. The increasingly nervous looking captive began to babble. "Jesu. I... I am sorry, sirs, forgive me. Forgive me, do. Maddocks is a terror, they say."

"Out with it, man," Lyle snapped. "It is getting dark and I am growing bored. What is your name?"

"Whistler, sir."

"Whistler."

The frightened fellow nodded rapidly. "On account of..."

Lyle interrupted him, "I have no doubt as to the provenance of the name. What do you do with yourself, Whistler, when you are not creeping about these hills?"

"I labour, sir." Whistler dug one of the remaining fingers of his right hand under the edge of his hat and scratched his temple. "Have dug ditches, knapped flint and worked the salt pans down at Hayling. Anything will serve, long as it puts food in my belly."

"Including thievery." Lyle looked directly at the mutilated appendage. "Not your first offence, either."

"Only when I have no other recourse," Whistler opined, unable to keep his eyes from straying between Lyle's sword and firearm. "I am hungry. What is a man to do?"

What indeed, thought Lyle, as he smothered the pang of hypocrisy that rose like damp through his bones. He told himself that his own crimes were of an altogether different substance. One of vengeance rather than simple larceny. Somehow innately more righteous. But, looking at the pathetic creature before him – drenched, hungry and frightened – he could not help but think that no man's circumstances were ever truly simple. “Where are you headed?” he asked eventually, filing the sharper edges from his tone.

“Portsmouth,” Whistler said, exploring his armpit with his complete hand in search of an unseen louse. “There to seek work.”

Except that possession of all five digits did not necessarily make Whistler's left hand any more useful. Lyle saw the scarring on the palm and ordered the man to hold it up. “What happened there?”

“A burn,” Whistler mumbled, keeping the raised fist balled.

“A brand,” Lyle replied.

Behind him, Spendlove enquired, “As punishment? Theft again?”

Lyle shook his head. He had caught a better glimpse before Whistler had grown wise to the scrutiny. Now, as he considered the doleful fellow without the focus upon his attempted robbery, he saw the man behind the misdeed. “That cap,” he pointed at Whistler's head, “is a Montero. An infantryman's staple. See the flaps folded down against the ears? Useful as a blazing hearth on a long winter's march. Open your hand fully, Whistler.”

The fingers slowly peeled back, staying curved like talons. It was clear the palm could never again become entirely flat. Spendlove stepped closer. “What is that mark?”

“Desertion,” Lyle answered grimly, for he had seen such marks before. Whistler's hand had been placed on a tray of red-hot iron that was shaped like a glove and had been branded for all the world to see. A symbol of punishment but also of ownership. The fingers were covered with small blemishes, like smallpox scars, where searing metal studs had pressed against the flesh. The palm, however, bore far more elaborate markings. “Note the letters 'C' and 'R',” Lyle said, “either side of the crown emblem?”

Spendlove looked up at him open-mouthed. "Carolus Rex?"

Lyle nodded. "King Charles." He asked Whistler, "A Cavalier, then?"

Whistler inspected his blighted palm for a second, before confirming, "Sir Allen Apsley's."

"Foot?"

"Pike."

"What happened?"

Whistler's bottom lip trembled in the hoary gloom. "I were a'feared." His eyes glazed as they peered into the past. "You cannot know what it was like."

"I know well enough," Lyle replied. "When did you run?"

"After Hinton Ampner," Whistler said, his voice a monotone, still immersed in a flood of memory.

"Hinton Ampner?" Lyle echoed incredulously, for it was a place he knew well. A tiny hamlet on the Winchester road and seat of one Sir John Hippesley, a Roundhead during the civil wars, whose rebellion against the crown had paid dividends under the Protectorate. Only last year Lyle had visited Hippesley's grand house, there to infiltrate a masquerade in order to steal an important document. But it was not a country manor that had made Whistler abandon his post and Lyle recalled the name of the next village situated on that busy highway. "Cheriton," he said. "There was a battle at Cheriton. Parliament took the field."

Spendlove nodded sagely. "I remember it well. The rebel news-sheets made much of it."

Lyle frowned at Whistler. "You must have been very young."

"Too damned young," Whistler replied with the ghost of a shudder.

"It is often thus." And Lyle could not prevent his own mind tumbling back through the years to a little place in the Northamptonshire wilderness. A place called Naseby. He had been sixteen, green as cabbage and frightened as a spring leveret. The blinding smoke, the stinking sulphur, the screams of grown men, the hoof-shaken ground and the heart-stopping drums. He had held his nerve. Kept the line. Followed orders and ignored the stench of his own piss as it warmed his breeches. Naseby had been hell on Earth. How close had he come to raking spurs into his mount's flesh and bolting for the hills?

Whistler swallowed thickly, his Adam's apple bobbing in that reedy neck. “My chin needed no blade. My voice high as a woman's. The guns. Jesu but they were loud. So loud.”

“You retreated in good order,” Lyle said, dredging up what detail he could from the back of his mind.

“The king's men, for certain,” Whistler's reply was rueful. “But not I. I dived right under a hawthorn hedge, curled up like a new-born pup. No one noticed me. Not even the Roundheads as they swept through. Night fell, I was alone. Freezing my stones off but breathing yet.”

“Never to return to Sir Allen's colour.”

“Or so I thought.” Whistler gave a wry smile. “Only to be snared like a coney outside Winchester.”

“You were recognised?”

Whistler nodded. "One of the prison guards claimed he knew my face. I swore blind they had the wrong fellow. How could he prove it? In the end it did not matter. The example was all.”

“Fortunate you were not hanged.”

“Fortunate? Maybe.”

Lyle sighed. He felt suddenly tired. With a jerk of his chin he indicated the way down to the road. “Begone, Whistler, before I change my mind.”

“Gone, sir?” Whistler echoed as though he were a halfwit. “Truly?” He pressed his mutilated hands together like a penitent. “By God, sir, you are the Samaritan from the Book of

Luke, leapt from the very pages. Nay, sir. An angel."

"Begone, sirrah," Lyle snapped, thrusting the pistol in its saddle holster, "before I deprive you of that yapping tongue too."

"I will." Whistler backed off, shuffling and bowing at the same time. He stooped to snatch up a threadbare snapsack from amongst the beech's roots. "That I will. I beg your forgiveness again."

Then he was gone, leaving Lyle and Spendlove standing beside the grey stallion, the only sound the hiss of rain on the canopy. The light was failing quickly now, darkness dimming the church to little more than an outline.

"You think me a hypocrite," Lyle said, impulsively wishing to deflect his old master's disapproval. "I take only from government men."

Spendlove shook his head. "I think you too soft, Samson."

Lyle gave a short grunt of laughter as he clambered into Star's saddle. "There but for the Grace of God, Master Spendlove. There but for the grace of God."

"It was God's grace that made you keep a loaded pistol."

Lyle grinned. "It wasn't loaded."

Spendlove's little pony, slopping bravely through roads that were now mere funnels of filth, made laborious work of hauling the trap and its rider up the hill to Chalton. The thatches of the village, nestled as it was amongst thick woodland, were all but invisible in the encroaching dusk but the square tower of St Michael and All Angels, one of the hamlet's two prominent structures, climbed over the swaying branches to guide them home.

The second noteworthy building could be heard before it was seen. The Red Lion, a tavern situated opposite the church on the far side of a triangular patch of lawn, was Chalton's beating heart. Like most of the surrounding homes it was a marriage of timber and thatch, though much larger than its neighbours, with rain-streaked windows all aglow and smoke tumbling thick from the chimneystack to mingle with the brooding sky and fragrance the air. The sounds of music and of laughter drifted down to them as they climbed, the weary traveller's siren song.

Lyle gave Star a final, gentle word of encouragement. The stallion, forced to drop pace to keep with the much smaller pony, snorted irritably, a spray of raindrops jetting from his muzzle. Lyle laughed. He breathed deep, letting the heady odour conjure warmth in his mind though there was none in his body. Water dripped from his hood as he rode, tapping rhythmically on the leather tops of the tall riding boots. Star shivered and he reassured his old companion with a soft voice and a patted neck.

"It is a dangerous game you play," Spendlove muttered as they drew up in the tavern's muddy yard. Two young lads, thin as whippets, dashed out from the shelter of a timber lean-to and took the horses' bridles.

Lyle slid from his saddle, boots immediately enveloped by the squelching mire. He pulled the double-barrelled pistol from its holster and delved in one of the saddlebags to fetch his wide-brimmed hat, then asked, "How often do you see soldiers in these parts?"

The boy holding Star peered up so that rain streaked his cheeks, eyes widening at the sight of the gun. "Not for weeks, m' lord."

Lyle looked at Spendlove. "You see?" He handed each boy a penny, then pulled back his hood and replaced it with the hat.

"I do not like it," Spendlove protested as they watched the lads unhitch the pony and coax both beasts to the stables.

"All shall be well," Lyle said, then caught Spendlove's pointed glance as he set about loading the pistol. He winked.

"Just in case."

They entered the tavern as soon as Star and his new companion were safely ensconced in the stable block, a muggy, steaming collection of buildings that stank of horseflesh, hay and dung. The stallion had whickered at their backs in disgruntlement until the ostler, lurking out of the rain, had produced a sack of fodder, seemingly from thin air, clicking his tongue in some secret equine language that immediately compelled Star to settle. Lyle had shaken his head, produced more coins, sworn at the fussy beast and left.

The taproom was stifling, the blast of hot air assailing Lyle the moment he stepped onto the chalk floor's blanket of fresh rushes. Fragments of convivial chatter had drifted out on the heat, like leaves tumbling on an autumn gust but they faded as abruptly as the music, a dozen pairs of eyes searching the doorway anxiously.

"Major-General Goffe's responsibility," Spendlove said, "not only encompasses the suppression of Royalist sympathy but charges him with the reformation of public manners."

Lyle nodded but held his peace. It was safer not to explain that the protective guise he donned since returning from France was that of an innkeeper. In that role he saw at first hand the moral expectations to which the people of the fledgling Commonwealth were held. Ever since Cromwell had divided England and Wales into ten regions, each to be governed by one of his military grandees, the government's efforts to make the nation Godlier had become considerably more concerted, enforced now at sword-point as well as pulpit. Of course, the excessive imbibing of strong drink could not be stamped out altogether, any more than Goffe might end dancing or laughter but if drunkenness was detected, penalties could be harsh and swift. That was why every one of the Red Lion's patrons was nervous of strangers. Any new face could be that of a government informant.

"And that is why," Spendlove went on, nodding at a figure slumped on a low stool beside the window, "Rotten Jeremiah, there, takes picket duty."

Lyle cast his gaze over the wizened old man who had apparently been playing lookout. The fellow's face was so deeply lined that it looked like the shell of a walnut, while from his mouth dangled a long, cold pipe. His eyes were firmly shut. "If he were my lookout," he said sardonically, "I would have him shot."

Spendlove, apparently unaware of Rotten Jeremiah's less than attentive efforts, had already moved to the counter, where a couple of locals, relaxing now that they recognised one of their own, patted his back and shared murmured condolences. He caught the tapster's attention with a polite cough. "Wine, if you please, John."

Lyle went to join his friend, weaving through the tobacco fug, skirting tables, two sleeping dogs and a mangy looking cat. The brick hearth was away to his left, blackened spit-dogs flanking its flames, the chimney breast above adorned with an assortment of iron shears.

"Wardley Spendlove," the tapster was saying, "a warm welcome to you." He was a portly man in his mid-forties, with short, lank hair the colour of slate. "I was deep afflicted to hear the news of dear Ursula. Young Botolph ain't been the same these past days."

"Thank you, John," Spendlove said. He put a hand to Lyle's shoulder. "An old acquaintance, come for the funeral. He would share a cup with me in her memory."

John gave them both an earnest nod and jabbed a gnarled thumb in the direction of two nearby barrels. "Sack or Malmsey, sirs."

The older man deferred to Lyle, who indicated that Malmsey and John went to work. Spendlove turned his back to the counter, propping elbows on the sticky surface and pointedly cast his gaze upon the Red Lion's tosspot, who was snaking from table to table, gathering spent trenchers, blackjacks and pots. "Botolph. Not as you recall, I'd wager."

"No," Lyle agreed, watching the lad work. Botolph Spendlove, whom he had known as a flaxen-haired and knock-kneed stripling, was now a strapping youth of stocky frame and square jaw. A grown man, to all intents and purposes. Yet still his face retained the freshness of childhood, a patchy beard of auburn fluff, the same shade as the thatch on his head, doing nothing to add to his fifteen years. "He has become a fine fellow, Master."

Spendlove flashed a proud smile. "Has his mother's looks."

"And he works here?"

"To earn us a few pennies. He and his sister, both. Times are not easy. But we persist. I tutor the youngsters hereabouts, Botolph and Amelia clear the pots and tend the taps."

Lyle watched Botolph attempt to scoop up one too many cups, promptly dropping one that clattered noisily to the ground. "And his ailment?"

Spendlove shrugged. "Half as many hands makes life twice as hard. But he manages."

"Wardley Spendlove!" a large, sweaty patron at one of the tables suddenly exclaimed. He did not stand, the glazed look in his eyes providing explanation but he raised a dented pewter goblet in salute, slopping claret over the table. "My prayers are with you, sir! Goodwife Spendlove was one of a kind." He paused, quaffing the wine and belching prodigiously. "Now she rests with God for eternity. We were all of us the better for having known her."

"Thank you," Spendlove acknowledged.

"I see why this place requires a picket line," Lyle said dryly, making his former teacher laugh.

"Father," Botolph said, startling them. He had evidently been roused to their presence by the drunken toast and now came to address both men with a concerned frown. "Did you walk? I told you not to. The roads are dangerous and..."

"I escorted your father, young sir," Lyle said, "have no fear."

Botolph's brows knitted further together. He drew up his shoulders and, Lyle noticed, let his palsied hand slip behind his back. "And you are?"

"A friend of mine, Botolph," Spendlove said in a soothing tone. "An old friend."

"Thomas Smith," Lyle invoked the first name to form on his tongue. "When last I saw you," he whistled softly, "zounds, you were barely knee high to a palfrey."

Botolph seemed to relent, stepping back slightly. "Grown now, Goodman Smith."

"Indeed." Lyle extended his hand. "And well met."

Botolph grasped Lyle's palm, though he kept his ruined left hand concealed. "A friend of father's is a friend of mine, sir."

"Here," Lyle said, passing his Malmsey to Botolph and ordering a replacement for himself. "Join us." They went to the nearest empty table and sat down. Out the corner of his eye, Lyle noticed a small service door at the furthest reach of the room. It opened and closed like a yawning mouth, the gathering night visible beyond. A young woman, wearing an apron over a corn coloured dress, came and went, rolling hogsheads through from what was, presumably, a storehouse in the yard. "It seems the tapster is not short on supplies."

Botolph smiled. "Delivery came in last evening, before the rain, thank the Lord." Beginning to relax, he sipped from the cup, then said, "Might I ask how you are acquainted?"

"Your father was my schoolmaster," Lyle explained, "when I

was but a snipe."

"Yours and many others."

"Right enough," Lyle agreed. "A grand man. His wife a grand woman. Showed me kindness that I shall never forget. That is why I have come." The new wine appeared and Lyle raised his cup and his voice. "To Ursula Spendlove, may she rest in Paradise."

Father and son joined the toast, as did half a dozen more across the room, their voices echoing amongst the blackened beams.

And then the strangers burst in.

Cold, damp air howled through the tavern, heralding the silhouettes that filled the doorway. Rotten Jeremiah was awake now, roused by the violence of the door slamming back to torture its hinges and he staggered to his feet, pipe skittering off his shoe, swaying wildly and spluttering a warning as incoherent as it was worthless.

"There!" the foremost silhouette snarled. "There's the villain!" His voice was guttural and harsh, the English stilted, unnatural, an accent borne thousands of miles to the east. "Duncan, Louis; take hold of the wretch!"

The night descended into chaos. More dark shapes forced their way over the threshold, breaking either side of the first man like streams about a boulder, gargoyle grimaces given life by shadow and candle-flame. Bcfore anyone could react, the most advanced pair had kicked up the rushes on their way to Lyle's table, taking young Botolph Spendlove in hand and wrenching him to his feet. At their backs, blocking the doorway, more men came in single file. All were powerfully built, scabbards conspicuous at their waists.

Lyle instinctively glanced at the little service door but knew he could not hope to make it before he was overrun. Instead he held his nerve and his peace, trying to identify the newcomers before he did anything rash. They might have been soldiers of some kind, he supposed. They wore no uniforms, no plate armour or field signs, which made him doubt whether they were members of the Protectorate's irresistible military wing, yet to encounter sell-swords in the tranquil Hampshire hills seemed just as unlikely. Duncan and Louis, the vanguard, loomed over his table, shoring up the helpless Botolph like twin buttresses. He could see daggers and pistols jammed into their belts. The larger, Duncan, had the youthful aspect of one just touching his twenties. He was pale-skinned and red-headed, a wide cross-belt bracing his torso, around which was coiled a knotted whip. His compatriot might have been a decade older, with a fastidiously-trimmed and oiled beard that could not entirely conceal skin blighted by scabies. Both men wore high boots but no spurs, setting him to wonder whether they travelled on foot. The ripe stench of leather, sweat, ale and tobacco wafted liberally from them.

While the highwayman mulled his distinctly sparse choices, Wardley Spendlove decided to act. "What is the meaning of this?" he cried as his stool shot out from under him, clattering to the chalk floor as he lunged for his son.

The surly men gripping Botolph by the arms swatted Spendlove contemptuously away, one of them putting a boot to his rump for good measure. The old man careened headlong, flailing almost comically, to sprawl amongst chair legs. His persecutors guffawed; loudly, cruelly.

But the laughter died as rapidly as it had begun. The girl came from nowhere. Not nowhere, thought Lyle; but from the shadows at the back, near the crates and the pots and the yard, where the candles had not been lit and the hearth's flames made few inroads. From the modest service door that led to the storehouse and its casks. It was the girl he had seen bringing in the barrels, dirty apron strung at waist, yellow sleeves pushed up to her elbows, mind bent only to her work. Except here she was, standing tall, having inveigled herself into the midst of the standoff entirely unobserved, to snatch the whip from Duncan's belt. She snarled like a trapped wolf, lashing at the whip's owner with the knotted leather so that he released Botolph and shrunk back, clutching his face with his hands. Blood seeped through his latticed fingers as he roared English obscenities mixed with a stream of Scots Gaelic that echoed in the rafters. She drew back the whip again, turning on the bearded man who still held the boy firm and her coif, scraped by her passing forearm, fell away, long tresses of dark brown hair tumbling in its wake. Blades appeared from behind the bearded man, brandished by his comrades to glint in the soft light. Some of them grinned, enjoying the spectacle but the threat was clear enough. Knowing she had failed, the girl stalled, breathing heavily as she let her arm drop, though she kept a tight grip on the whip. Duncan took hold of Botolph again, spitting another vicious oath at her. There was a thin, red gash across his chin.

That was when Lyle stood up. He pulled the pistol from his waistband and levelled it, not at Botolph's captors but at their leader, who was no longer a featureless silhouette but a broad, tall, ruddy-faced and thickly moustachioed menace, with a feathered hat in one hand, his other resting on the sword pommel at his hip. Lyle retreated by a half-dozen paces, putting distance between himself and the strangers. The girl immediately fell back too, seizing the opportunity to move into the space he had created.

The leader of the armed men looked coolly at them both. His bright blue eyes sharpened at the metallic clunk of Lyle's pistol, the hammer thumbed back into the cocked position but he did not flinch, save the shifting of one cheek as it was wrinkled by a mordant smirk. He eyed the firearm. "A pretty piece. What kind of man might brandish such a thing?"

Lyle kept the weapon steady. The foreigner's florid complexion was blemished further by the pale white lines of aged scars and he picked one, a deep divot below the left eye, on which to train the muzzle. "The man who will kill you." He spoke truthfully, for, unlike at Idsworth, the weapon really was primed and ready to fire. There was always a risk that the rain had spoiled the charge, for black powder attracted moisture like the driest sponge imaginable but he was willing to gamble that Botolph's captors would not be eager to put it to the test.

The man with the bushy whiskers licked his lips slowly, gauging the scene. "Two bullets."

Lyle nodded, retiring a couple of paces further. "For two men." He twitched the muzzle so it roved over the figures gathered in the doorway, a barricade of steel and flesh that would be impossible to breach. "You may choose, if it please."

The ruddy fellow canted his head to the side, as if deciding whether Lyle were short of wits. A golden hoop glittered in his right earlobe. "There are eleven of us, *Skurwysyn*."

"Then you will leave as nine." It was all Lyle could do to keep the pounding of his heart from manifesting as a trembling hand. "Is the boy worthy of such a price?"

"Is he worth your life?"

"Aye," Lyle answered. For the first time, he noticed the expression on Botolph's face. One of bafflement as much as fear. He realised, too, that the girl with the whip was looking at him with curiosity and now he truly saw her. Or, rather, he saw her mother in the face looking up at him. This was Ursula Spendlove's daughter, Amelia. She had the same dark brown eyes, brightened by touches of ochre that caught the candlelight like flakes of gold. The same wide mouth that gave her a serious, solemn countenance and the same petite figure that belied undoubted boldness.

Forcing himself to turn back to the man with the moustache, he said, "Well? How is this night to end?"

Silence hung heavy as a sodden robe. Lyle held firm, despite the aching of the wound in his back, wondering which of them would make the first move. These were hard men, any fool could see, utterly accustomed to violence. All it would take was a word, perhaps a mere gesture, from their leader and the Red Lion would be awash with smoke and blood. And yet something had given the foreigner pause. He had not anticipated resistance in this bucolic idyll, let alone outright threat and, as Lyle had hoped, he clearly harboured no wish to weaken his party on account of a spotty-faced tosspot.

After what seemed like an eternity, the moustachioed man cleared his throat to speak. "We want what is ours, nothing more." The corner of his wide mouth fluttered, the chasm in his cheek deepening. "And nothing less."

"Yours?" Lyle said. He stepped back again. Close enough now, perhaps, to bolt for the rear door. But could he leave the Spendloves at the mercy of these men?

"A treasure." The glassy blue gaze slid to regard Botolph, who dangled between the armed men like a doe's carcass. "Stolen by this knave." His hard voice dropped lower as contempt crept in. "This dead man."

Botolph thrashed at that, the precariousness of his situation finally crystallising in his mind. He received Duncan's backhand, swift and savage, for his trouble and went immediately limp.

Amelia Spendlove looked as though she would lash out again with the whip but halted when Lyle shouted, "He is just a boy!"

"My boy!" Wardley Spendlove, still felled but sitting up now, was covered in the filth of the floor. He sobbed pitifully as he cradled an elbow, tears sketching pale lines through the grime of his cheeks.

"Father," Amelia whispered. She dropped the whip and, all bluster gone, went to crouch beside the prone old man, weeping as he wept.

The moustache flinched, climbing on one side of its owner's face to reveal brilliant white teeth.

Lyle caught the look. One he knew all too well. "Come here, girl."

Botolph's sister glanced up at him, a mix of bewilderment and anger passing like a storm cloud over her face. "I think not, sir."

"Damn it all, Amelia, do as you are goddamned told!"

She flinched at that, then her sombre, earnest expression hardened into something more defiant and Lyle privately berated himself for the outburst. But Wardley was muttering with soft urgency in her ear and, to his surprise, she was kissing her father on the forehead and clambering to her feet. Without a word she came to stand behind Lyle.

Wardley Spendlove had not taken his eyes off his son. "He is my good Christian boy. Never has he hurt a soul."

The scarred man's half smile transformed into a sneer that was brimming with scorn. "I was younger than this whelp when I took my first life."

"As was I," Lyle responded as the Naseby drums boomed in his mind. "Providence conspires against us at times but that does not grant licence to torment every youth you see fit." He risked another glance at Botolph, whose wretched face had taken on the milky hue of the condemned. Wine-dark blood welled from an artificially flared nostril. "You accuse this boy of theft?"

"I do."

"When was this crime committed?"

"Yesterday," the man with the moustache said, taking a step further into the room. He wore a long cassock, the brass buttons glimmering in time with the hoop in his ear. The acolytes at his back shifted their feet, growling in low threat, evidently eager to take whatever revenge had been promised and planned. "At the big farm to the south of Petersfield."

"Yesterday?" Wardley Spendlove echoed indignantly. "My son was here." His voice faltered and cracked with the strain of the moment. "His mother passed away this last week. He has barely left our home, let alone the village."

That seemed to jar with the hitherto unyielding foreigner. He licked his lips slowly, eyes shifting from one face to the next as if he tried to read each mind in turn. "We have tracked our hare over the hills," he said eventually. "Followed his every footstep. We had a witness."

"Had?" Lyle asked pointedly.

Duncan, huge and malevolent at Lyle's left flank, flashed a dark, toothless grin of unholy relish. "The piglet did squeal," he said in a querulous tone that was incongruous set against an accent made in the Scots lowlands. "Oh yes he did." He gave the semi-conscious Botolph a jolt, like a hound shaking a rabbit. It elicited a soft, forlorn groan. "The piggy did identify this rogue as our quarry and that he did."

Lyle shook his head. "It cannot be. You are mistaken."

The man with the moustache caressed his sword pommel with the palm of his left hand. "I think it is you who are gravely mistook, *Skurwysyn*." He cocked his head like a curious dog. "Who are you, that you would court death in this manner? Soldier?"

"A soldier in an army of one," Lyle answered.

"Brigand, then?"

Closer to the mark than you realise, thought Lyle. "Will you release the boy?"

The foreigner lifted his feathered hat and placed it atop his head. A benign enough gesture, except that it freed up his right hand, with which he carefully drew back the cassock to reveal a large-handled pistol and the fat haft of a small axe. The sword, more fully visible now, appeared to be curved, broadening as it swept away from the hilt. "My name is Marek."

"Prussian?" Lyle said, stalling and planning in the same instant, bracing himself for a fight even as he prepared to leap for the door.

"Polish," Marek answered and he seemed to take a pause, as if anticipating recognition. When none came, he said, "But you can call me death, *Skurwysyn*."

Lyle chose not to enquire as to the meaning of the final term; the intended insult was clear enough. "Death, then," he replied, deliberately blasé to hide the chill that played at his neck. "Why are you here?"

"All you need to know, *Skurwysyn*, is that I *am* here and I will have my property, or the boy will die."

"You are footpads," Lyle said. "Outlaws. If you spill blood the Army will hunt you down."

Marek grinned. "And who will raise the hue and cry? You? A man who sups beneath a hat slanted to hide his face? You are unlikely to scuttle to the authorities, I suspect."

"You will get nothing from him," Lyle protested, desperate now, for he could see a night of frustration for Marek that could only culminate in the agonies of others. Botolph's innocence would achieve nothing but condemn him to a slower death.

Marek's smile widened. "Do not concern yourself, *Skurwysyn*. We have done this before. Why don't you take a seat and watch?"

*

Havant, Hampshire

Night was Whistler's friend. His ally. It was the time he came alive. Time for him to go to work. It was deep into the smallest hours and Havant slept. He had hoped for darker skies but the storm-clouds had inched inland at the harrying of the Solent's biting winds and the moon had revealed itself to give road, tree and rooftop a wan outline. Whistler, though, had learned to count his blessings. At least it was no longer raining.

Tugging down the flaps of his Montero cap to bring warmth to his ears and cheeks, he rubbed the ruined palm of his left hand with the mutilated nubs of his right, then edged out onto the road. A dog barked and he hesitated, shrinking back into the mouth of the alley from whence he had emerged but nothing came of the brief commotion. He checked the street again, before cautiously venturing forth.

It had taken almost three hours to reach the town, by way of rain-sluiced tracks that had cloyed at his every step in a concerted attempt to swallow his shoes. If his belly had been full then he would never have attempted the hazardous journey. If the confounded horseman at Idsworth chapel had not returned to his mount when he did, Whistler would have had an array of useful goods to sell. A trip to one of the taverns at Chalton, Finchdean or Rowlands Castle would undoubtedly have revealed some ostler or farmhand far enough into his cups to be parted with a few coins. A groat or two for a tinderbox, perhaps more for a powder flask or, better still, a nice saddle cloth. The transaction would have yielded enough for a meal and board. A place beside the fire. If he had managed to snatch the pistol or the exquisite war hammer, he would be set for the rest of winter. But it was not to be. The horseman, whoever he was, had been implacable. Frightening, even. Those cold green eyes had chilled Whistler to the marrow and he had known that it was enough simply to escape with his life.

So it was south that he had headed. He had told the green-gazed villain that Portsmouth was his goal and he supposed that was true, in a roundabout way, though he had little intention to seek honest employment within its fortress walls. But the harbour town was too far for one night's trudge and so he would make do with Havant, a couple of miles to the east of Portsmouth, at least until sun-up. And Havant was a plump goose to pluck, if ever there was one. A settlement that had sprung up around a road built by the Romans but that had truly flourished by dint of its natural springs. Water mills had been constructed here, with tanneries and breweries and all manner of manufacturing, so that the place, given its relatively modest size, was as rich as any outside of London. Whistler was cold, he was sodden and his stomach was so empty that it convulsed excruciatingly. But he knew that his stars were about to change. He was a fox in the proverbial hen house.

From the shadows at the road's fringe, he scanned the premises on the far side. Immediately opposite was a large tavern. The lure of the heady woodsmoke meandering from its trio of chimneys had been nothing short of a taunt for one without a single coin to his name. He could hardly loiter before the warming flames without purchasing a single drink, for the result would be a thick ear and a charge of vagrancy that would see him land a spell in the stocks or lashed to the whipping post. Thus, he had skulked in his alley during the late evening, jealously observing the rowdy establishment as the candles flickered in the windows, silhouettes of drinkers passing to and fro beyond. He had listened to the desolate moans of the dancing bear tethered to a stake in its yard, heard the laughter of men tossing coins at the pathetic animal as it sauntered for their pleasure and breathed the aroma of sot weed smoke, freshly baked bread and meat pies. All as the rain had come down, cruel and unrelenting.

Whistler had still been in his alleyway as the candles had finally guttered and the tavern's patrons filtered out onto the street, bound for home. Shutters had clacked into place all along the street, doors locked and barred. The sorrowful bear had ceased his call, presumably led away to see out the night in a cage. Whistler had waited patiently as the watchmen completed their rounds, calling the hour as they strode Havant's main crossroads by the light of swaying lanterns. They hummed tunes and spat tobacco as they paced, in pairs and threes, nodding to the last of the folk they encountered, reminding the citizenry of whatever new laws Major-General Goffe had deigned important.

He had still been there when silence had fallen and the clouds had lifted. Now the town was his alone.

*

Chalton, Hampshire

"What did your witness say?" Lyle's pistol was still trained on the men crowding the end of the taproom nearest the tavern's door. "Will you not reveal the charge, sirrah, so that this poor wretch might offer some defence?"

The Pole's smile coloured all but his eyes. "I am no magistrate, *Skurwysyn* and this is no court of law."

"Nor are you an executioner."

Marek inclined his head. "Very well. The answer lies in the hand." He turned his brutal face on the younger Spendlove. Duncan, the Scot, lifted Botolph's arm like a trophy. At the end of that limb, dangling like a limp flag, was the palsied hand, palm enclosed by fingers unnaturally curled inwards like the petals of a desiccated flower.

Lyle remembered the anguish of Wardley and Ursula Spendlove when first the afflicted babe had come screaming into the world. At the fear that their beloved son would suffer more than just deformed flesh when the fullness of time revealed the person he would become. He remembered, too, the whispers of the gossips, the greybeards' censorious glances and the open mockery of other children.

Marek was pointing at the hand. "The man I seek bears Satan's mark."

"His hand?" Lyle scoffed. "That is all? It contracts of its own accord. Has done since birth. A common enough disorder." To a man, Marek's company sketched crosses before their chests. The act was so brazen that it took Lyle aback and he heard himself say, "Papists?" The men did not answer but his mind was already putting the gesture together with the curved swords and the lack of military insignia. "You're sailors."

"Perceptive as well as suicidal," Marek said.

The attack came from the right flank. A short, strongly built man with a shaven scalp, an amber-toothed grimace and pock-pitted skin lunged out of the shadows. In his white-knuckled fist flashed a long, slender dagger, driving up and out from the hip, bound for the soft space immediately beneath Lyle's ribcage. At Amelia's warning shout, Lyle took one, two, three rearward paces, offering only air for the blade to slice. As his assailant flailed and overstepped, he drew his rapier with his free hand in one swift motion, the hiss loud beneath the low ceiling as it slid from the scabbard. With a staccato forward step, as if dancing a Galliard, he flicked his wrist and the sword's delicate tip darted upwards, just brushing the side of the shorter man's hand. The fellow recoiled, yelping as he let the knife drop to the floor. All the while, the pistol's twin muzzles kept level with Marek and his bunched comrades, so that no one else moved.

The tapster, cowering back against his hogsheads, gasped. "God save us, it is…" he began, then swallowed back whatever exclamation had begun to form.

All was still. Lyle steadied his frenzied heart and gritted his teeth against the pain in his shoulder blade, the scab encrusted wound leaving him in no doubt as to whether it had fully healed.

But Marek was looking at the tapster now. "What were you going to say?"

The grey-haired man opened and shut his mouth like a dying fish, stuffing his hands into the pockets of his apron. "Nowt, m'lord, honest."

Marek unsheathed his own sword now. Slowly, purposefully. He was close to the tapster, so Lyle could do nothing to intervene and he raised the blade above the height of the counter, letting the tip hover in line with the frightened man's belly like a poised serpent. "Use your tongue or lose it."

The tapster raised a trembling hand to point at Lyle. "I… I seen him afore, m'lord. Tis the Ironside Highwayman hi'self."

Only then did Lyle realise that, in the brief scuffle, his hat had shunted back and up, tilting away to shade his neck instead of his face. His heart sank just as Marek's brow rose.

"Ironside?" the Pole quizzed the room.

"Cavalry, m'lord," the tapster mumbled fearfully.

Marek's eyes did not move from Lyle. "Now your twinkling swordplay is explained."

Lyle shook his head. "I took instruction from Charles Besnard." He had been hiding in the Paris fencing school, of course. Grieving and recovering and learning by turns. But no one in this place needed to know that.

Marek whistled softly. "A master," he said in what appeared to be genuine admiration. "My compliments."

"The ironsides," one of his company interjected from the back of the armed group, the accent's hard vowels unmistakably the product of Ulster, "were Cromwell's goddamned horsemen. Murdering villains, all." He pushed his way to the front so that he could see Lyle. "Tell me. Were you in Ireland?"

"Hush," Marek ordered. "He may dress like a cavalry officer

but that does not make him one." The corner of his mouth upturned in a sneer, animating his whiskers, as he appraised Lyle with new interest. "Highwayman? You are nothing but a thief. A ditch hider and a mask wearer and a coward."

"You know nothing," Lyle replied, all too aware that his tone lacked conviction. He was thinking of the thief at Idsworth and smarting at the irony of it all.

Marek's line of thought was straightening now, like a loosed arrow and he was not to be deterred. He laughed, loudly and mirthlessly, like a sudden thunderclap, then waved the sword at Botolph Spendlove. "He is in your employ."

"No," Lyle replied.

The exchange stirred Botolph, who brought up his head. "I've never seen him before tonight, I swear it."

A backhand from Louis clubbed him to silence. Wardley Spendlove, still prone, mewed like a wounded animal as fresh blood trickled from his son's mouth. Amelia started forwards but, to Lyle's relief, evidently thought better of it.

"This cursed creature," Marek was saying, pointing the steel at Botolph but keeping his glittering eyes on Lyle, "is your man. You are a renegade of these woods, *Skurwysyn* and he does your bidding. Why else would you be here? Why else would you intervene? You spoke of his Devil's hand, that you saw it when he was a baby."

"He stole nothing," Lyle protested, "and he knows me not."

"Why would you risk your life for his?" Marek made a tutting sound with his tongue. "Give me the treasure. End this foolishness."

"What is this treasure you have lost?"

"A book. A blessed book. But you know that already."

Lyle scanned the room for the dozenth time in search for a way to break the deadlock. He would not back down but nor could he give the man his treasure. The front entrance was well and truly blocked, while he would be hunted down by the sailors before he reached the rear door. He needed to stall for time while the wheels of his mind frantically spun. "The sailor's road passes near here," he blurted. "You're travelling from London, bound for ship at Portsmouth. Or the other way around."

Marek nodded. "The *Diamond*."

"Fourth-rater," Lyle said, dredging scraps of information from the back of his mind. "Forty guns. Part of Blake's fleet."

"Lately at Cadiz," Marek confirmed. "Returned home for refit and refreshment. My lads and I have been at Bankside," he shook his hip so that an unseen purse jangled with money, "at the prize play. Now we travel home. We will join the ship at Spithead on Friday."

Lyle risked a backward half-step. Marek's men flinched. The clicks of cocking hammers rang out in the gloom. He was stuck fast. Trapped like a fox in a snare. "Friday," he repeated the word. Time enough to act, he thought and a flash of memory cracked across his mind like Duncan's whip. "I do not have the book but I can get it for you."

Marek's eyes narrowed. He glanced at his bristling, glowering cohort, then at Botolph and finally let his gaze find its way back to Lyle. He pursed his lips in apparent contemplation. "You would strike a deal with me, *Skurwysyn*? You are brave, I give you that."

Lyle shrugged. "Do you want the book back or not? Kill us now and it is lost forever."

Nothing showed on the Pole's implacable face but his arm moved and the broad cutlass hissed its way into its scabbard. "Very well. You will return my property by the time we cast off, or this pathetic specimen will bathe in the Solent."

"He is a good swimmer."

"Even when hogtied? Truly, the boy must be kinsman to Poseidon himself." Marek spat at Botolph's feet, inching closer to Lyle. “Please understand me, Ironside Highwayman. You and your associate have stolen something very dear to me. To us. We have run our quarry to ground, praise the Holy Mother and the devil-touched whoreson will come south with us at sun-up. Either our property is returned by the time we depart for Spithead, or he dies. You have my word on it.”

*

Havant, Hampshire

Whistler scampered across the street, leaping glassy puddles and piles of horse-dung as he went. Hunger made him weak but it also made him resolute. The buildings on this side of the road were principally involved with animal skins. A tannery, a fellmonger and purveyors of vellum and ink all had their place. But the jewel in Havant's crown was the large parchmenter's premises that devoured the lion's share of the row and it was beneath its deeply jettied first floor that Whistler came to a halt. He pressed his back against one of the massive double doors, high and broad like those of a tithe barn, as he paused to catch his breath. The site was one of bustling industry during the day but now all was still, the gates firmly shut and barred and the challenge would be a matter of finding a way into the imposing building. When he had composed himself, he slid along the door, always searching the road for the return of the watchmen or prying eyes in overlooking windows. Nothing gave him undue alarm, so he continued until his shoulder blade felt the scrape of the building's corner. He rounded it, always facing outward, finding himself in a new passageway as he stumbled over a discarded hogshead, rotten beyond repair and slid along the gable wall. In and out he breathed, footsteps silent, craning his neck so that he could check for suitable features in the wall.

Like magic, it resolved from the gloom about a yard above his head. A rectangular ventilation grate, cut into the wall between two of the timber stanchions and sealed by a grid of metal bars. It was tiny, barely a square foot in dimension. A child would have struggled to fit through it. Except that it had rained all day.

Whistler returned to the broken hogshead and dragged it through the mud until it was positioned beneath the grate. He climbed, gingerly at first and bobbed his knees a couple of times to test its durability. Despite an alarming chorus of creaks and cracks, it held firm and he pulled a rusty and much-used chisel from his snapsack. Glancing over both shoulders, he jammed the sharpened point into the wall. The building's timber frame might have been stout but the spaces between the great oaken joists were made of wattle and caked in daub. The daub – a mixture of clay, straw, mud and chalk dust – had been whitewashed, to improve both the aesthetic and its resistance to rain. But it had rained a great deal and, while the wall was not about to melt into the gutter, it was soft enough to offer only meagre resistance to a chisel wielded by a tenacious hand. It took Whistler less than a minute to excavate the outer layer of daub into which the grate had been sunk and it came away with a concerted tug.

He placed the metal fixing carefully on the ground and peered through the hole. All was dark, too dark to take an effective inventory but that hardly mattered. He knew well enough that the open-plan space would hold the accoutrements of an industry delivering prodigious wealth to the town. Stone vats, containing a solution of lime and water, in which the valuable pristine-white skins of South Downs sheep would be soaked for days at a time. Wooden structures upon which the slippery hides, fresh from soaking, would be draped, ready for the remnants of hair to be scraped clean to reveal the pink skin beneath. There would be containers holding bare, tidy skins that were scheduled to be rinsed in the fresh waters of the local springs, purged of lime residue so that they might next be stretched taut on frames for drying. There would be a trove of tools, too. Good quality items that might fit discreetly about a man's person. Easy to steal, easier to sell. But there was something extra special about this place. It teased a particular kind of treasure. One that had Whistler grinning in the desultory moon-glow and redoubling his efforts. His ruined hands screamed with the strain, though he swallowed back the pain, proximity to his prize acting as a salve.

With each movement of the chisel more clumps came away, spattering his sodden shoes, exposing the latticed wattle beneath like the bones of a flayed carcass. When there was enough of the woven hurdle on show, he simply pulled. Returning the chisel to the snapsack and gripping the ends of the coppiced hazel strips where they had been cut to form the setting for the grate, he hauled with all his might, letting his feet dangle to the sides of the hogshead so that his entire weight might contribute to the struggle.

One by one, the sticks broke. The noise was excruciating in the still of the night but intermittent moments of frozen, ear-pricked terror gave way to frenetic action as he gradually enlarged the hole, each splintering spar a word of encouragement. It was not long before the modest vent had become a man-sized window into which Whistler hauled himself, hooking elbows over the edge of the jagged gap, scrabbling with his toes for purchase against the wall, cursing the height and the sharp spears of hazel and the day’s foul weather and the green-eyed horseman whose earlier intervention had driven him to this. In moments his top half had slithered into the dry air on the far side of the wall, balanced by his waist on the fractured wattle like a seal about to launch from its rock into the surf. For a heart-stopping second, he feared he would be stranded there, snagged by his breeches on the split fronds but then the momentum shifted and down he went, plummeting into the shadowy abyss, arms outstretched, bracing against the unseen.

He hit the floor hard, rolled, clattered into something wooden that immediately toppled about him. But he laughed inwardly all the same. Because he was unhurt and he was inside.

He disentangled himself from the wooden structure that, with quickly adjusting eyes, he saw was a hoop-shaped frame, across which a pale skin was stretched, held firm by strings and pegs that could be altered to accommodate the inevitable shrinkage. He pulled the apparatus upright. The skin was rubbery and damp. It had been scraped to the blemish-free sheen of the latter stages of the process, left to dry before the final steps that would transform it into viable parchment.

More edges and lines resolved from the shadows as Whistler gauged his new surroundings. The vats were present as expected, flanked by tool benches, buckets and brooms. There were piles of finished skins, ready for cutting to shape and various crates and trunks that might have warranted investigation had time allowed. Shelves heaved with all manner of objects and hooks protruded from the high beams, from which dangled bunches of dried herbs that did valiant battle against the perpetual stench.

Whistler moved through the gloom, picking a silent path to the rear of the workshop, where three smaller doors implied rooms beyond. None was locked. He opened each in turn. The first was an office, perhaps that of the clerk. A Spartan environment inhabited by a huge table that was empty, save a jar of quills and two ink pots. There were a couple of chairs and a wide bookcase crammed and sagging with papers. He entered but only to quickly riffle through a drawer set into the table. Therein, he discovered a solid hunk of bread wrapped in an oily cloth and a scrap of some unidentifiable meat, dried and seasoned for longevity. He could have wept but staved off the pricking tears. He did not resist a breathless prayer of thanks. Then he crammed the lot into his mouth and closed his eyes as he savoured every morsel.

The second room was little more than a cupboard. A copse of tall brooms, boxes of bunched and balled cloths, some short-handled brushes and a collection of pails of various capacities. The third room, however, was the reason he was here. The reason he had especially chosen this factory in a town full of wealthy businesses. It was a storeroom. Lined all the way around its edge by solid chests, stacked three high, so that the top layer reached Whistler's chin. There were dozens and he could not hope to check the contents of them all, which was why it was a relief to know that what lay within each one was identical to the next. He simply went to the nearest and lifted the heavy lid, standing on tiptoes to peer inside.

Parchment. Pristine white gold, with the merest hint of yellow, made from Hampshire's coveted downland flocks and Havant's famous and mystical springs. This was the finished product; dried, cut, inspected, rolled and tied with ribbon, all ready to be transported to the four corners of the Commonwealth and beyond. Parchment was expensive and this stuff was the very best money could buy. Whistler unslung his snapsack and opened it wide, muttering thanks to the parchmenter for preparing his wares in such tidy and easily hidden scrolls. He allowed himself a smug smile, for this loot, when converted into coin down in Portsmouth by the hands of ship's captains and dockyard clerks, would see him through the winter.

When the bag was full, he closed the lid and turned. Which was when he was punched in the face.

WEDNESDAY

Near Rogate, Sussex

"I warned you not to go," the man muttered from high in the saddle as his black gelding negotiated sticky mire that had, until yesterday, been a firm trackway between dense gorse thickets. The horse snorted gently as if for answer, earning a patted neck, while its rider, as craggy and weather-beaten as his oversized buff-coat, continued unabashed. He craned his reedy neck sideways to address one of his two companions. "Did I not, girl? Don't go to Idsworth, says I, for some kestrel-eyed bastard'll know your face and trouble will surely follow. Is that not what I said?"

The girl in question, diminutive upon a bulky roan mare, seemed pained to agree but nodded nevertheless. "That's about the size of it."

The first man cackled triumphantly, revealing rotting gums that sprouted crooked, amber teeth. He was extremely thin, his coat hanging off his bony frame as though it had been draped over a broomstick and his shoulders were severely hunched, giving him the look of an ancient tree, bowing against the passage of time. His face was lined deep by years, furred in wintry white bristles and given a hawkish aspect by a long nose that was hooked and red at the tip. "But do he listen to old Eustace? Do he Hell. Now look." He cackled again, ruefully. "Shite on a short stick."

Behind the old man and young girl, Samson Lyle said, "My decision to pay my respects to Ursula Spendlove has no bearing upon our current predicament."

Eustace Grumm twisted all the way round to face him. "If you weren't at that God-forsaken ghost village, you would not have supped at Chalton."

The sun had not yet fully risen but a grey light showed the way as the narrow track joined an established bridleway, sunk deep over time, so that it was thickly fringed by brown bracken and bare lime trees.

"If he had not gone," a fourth voice spoke in the gloom, "my brother would have no hope at all." Amelia Spendlove, peering over Lyle's shoulder, fixed Grumm with a furious glare that made him turn quickly back to the bridleway. She rode pillion on Star's broad back, clutching tight at the highwayman's midriff. She had dispensed with the apron, replacing it with Lyle's spare coat against the cold, the hem of her skirts now brown with mud.

The trio of horses drew together as they eased watchfully out onto the cloying bridleway, collectively nervous of the peril posed by the wider road's high banks.

At the front, Grumm muttered, "And I'd be snug in my bed, none the wiser." He looked up as he spoke, scanning the darkly tangled boughs for signs of movement or the telltale glow of a slow match. Louder now, he said, "Not traipsing out through this bliddy muck and this bliddy cold."

"It is not that cold," Lyle said, running a gloved hand over Star's pricked ears as the animal took up position between the other mounts so that they travelled three-abreast. He studied the looming banks too. The thick blanket of rotting leaves, the gaping entrances to badger setts and the craters left by uprooted trees. It was a wolf-grey morning, the kind that could conceal all manner of danger. Crows cawed as they swirled high above, an unseen brook gurgled somewhere nearby but otherwise nothing stirred. He let a hand drop to the butt of his pistol all the same, reassured by its presence in the saddle holster. His arm pressed against Amelia's and he felt her tense. Withdrawing it quickly, he said, "And at least the rain has finally relented."

Before Grumm could muster what would doubtless have proved a less than sanguine response, Amelia cut in, "I would have no hope either."

Lyle's instinct was to play down her statement as hyperbole but they both knew he had saved her, despite her initial resistance, from the close attentions of Marek and his swash-and-buckler men. "You are safe now," he said.

"And you are certain that boy will find my father?"

Lyle nodded. "Young Hector is most reliable." When he and the girl had bolted for the little rear door and the yard beyond, leaving Wardley Spendlove on the tavern floor had been a wrench for them both. Yet Lyle had wanted someone trustworthy to remain and the old man had been the obvious – the only – choice. The first thing he had done, after riding Star into the rain-lashed night, was locate Hector, a shepherd's boy with the body of a seven year-old and the mind of the shrewdest card-sharp. "He'll find Master Spendlove and deliver the message."

"Tell it again, Samson," Bella said, with unapologetic relish. "These men were sailors?"

"With Blake's fleet, 'pon the *Diamond*."

"Thought the venerable General at Sea," Grumm sneered, "was down haranguing the Diegos."

"Blockading Cadiz," Lyle confirmed. "Part of the fleet has returned for a refit. This Marek and his lads have been enjoying the pleasures of Bankside during shore leave. He mentioned he had competed at the prize play and he certainly has the physique for it. Now they're returning to port." He cast his mind back to the previous night, replaying Marek's words. Seeing again the nonchalant brutality in that slab-like face, the predatory strength in his bearing. A chill formed on the surface of his skin. "They were hard sorts. Not common ruffians. Dangerous."

"And you have 'em riled," Grumm said bitterly. "Shite on a

short stick."

Bella glanced across at Lyle, her long, mousy hair falling over a face full of freckles. "Best you ran away, then."

Lyle winced at her choice of words. "Not a decision from which I derive a deal of pride, I assure you. But I struck a deal with Marek, which has bought us time."

"You should have stayed clear of the whole bloody show, if you ask me," Grumm commented.

The arms wrapped at Lyle's waist tightened a fraction. "You would have had him sit back and quaff his wine," Amelia retorted acerbically, "while those vile creatures tortured my little brother for a book he does not possess?"

Grumm harrumphed theatrically into Tyrannus's thick neck, declining to pick a fight. Lyle stifled a grin.

Bella said, "Your old school master got the stones to keep up with these sailors?"

"To protect his son?" Lyle replied. "Aye, I'd stake my life on it." And that had been the plan, such as it was. Hector had told Spendlove that he was to stay with Marek's men. Take his pony and trap and shadow them all the way south, so that Lyle would be free to fathom an answer to Botolph's sorry predicament. Once they reached the coast, Spendlove was charged with noting the location of the sailors' lodgings and then finding an old associate of Lyle's who could provide a safe house where he could sit tight. Lyle and Amelia, meanwhile, had galloped Star hard all the way back to the Ironside Highwayman's bolt-hole, a tavern on the edge of the village of Rake, there to rouse Bella and Grumm, his companions in life and accomplices on the road, just before the sun took a foothold on the eastern hills. Now they travelled south as the sodden fields crackled and the birds began their song.

Bella, who was around twelve, they reckoned – though the matter was oft debated – clicked her tongue in gentle encouragement as her horse negotiated a felled log. “What now?”

“We shan't attack them,” Lyle said. “I confess I had considered it.”

“I bet you had,” replied Grumm with dark amusement.

“Why not?” Bella asked, a lack of years never equating to a lack of courage. “The three of us can take them, can't we, Samson?” She glanced at Amelia, perhaps reflecting upon the tale she had heard regarding Duncan’s stolen whip and added, “Four of us.”

“I believe you could best anyone, truly,” Lyle said.

“Ambush them on the road,” she scoffed. “We know where they're headed.”

“Marek's men are not common bandits,” Lyle chided, though he could not stifle a laugh. In truth, while her bravado might one day be the end of her, he was proud of the indomitable young woman she had become. Dorothy Forks had been her name when first he had made her acquaintance. That meeting, on a thickly forested road not vastly dissimilar to the one on which they now travelled, had occurred by way of a proposition. Little Dorothy, a raggedy, snot-nosed snipe with a well-practised curtsy that was as coquettish as it was repellent, had stepped into Star's path and offered all manner of favours in return for a few coins. Her pimp had lurked nearby, propped against a knotted blackthorn as he monitored the exchange with hungry eyes. Lyle had promptly snapped the stick over its owner's pate, scooped the girl into the saddle and offered her a different life. She had thrown herself headlong into Lyle's strange existence, taking on the daylight guise of respectable alehouse mistress, while at night she played accomplice to the region's most notorious highwayman, all on the condition that Dorothy Forks would cease to exist.

Bella pulled a sour face. “Well I think we ought to fight.”

Grumm snorted. "We'd get ourselves killed, you daft mare."

"Tempting as it is," said Lyle, "we would not stand a chance. These are seasoned fighters, not green recruits."

"So are the Mad Ox's troopers," Bella countered, "and we best them all the time."

"This is different," Lyle answered levelly, conjuring this new adversary's image in his mind. The blue eyes twinkling from within that broad, florid face. The sardonic smile of neat, white teeth beneath that bristling upper lip. The cavernous scar blighting the man's cheek. He said, "The threat is real. I sense Marek and his company are capable."

"I'm glad it's not all wool in that skull o' yours," Grumm interrupted him brightly, evidently feeling an argument had been won.

"Yet I cannot leave him to the mercy of those men."

Now the old man wrenched himself about, glaring at Lyle with blazing eyes. "And I wonder if your wits have finally turned to suet, Major. You'd risk all our lives for a lad you barely knows?" He shifted his gaze to Amelia. "I am sorry, miss, it is a crying shame but-"

"You're in the right of it, Eustace," Lyle interrupted, "but his father and mother mean a great deal to me." And that fact was the axis about which his every thought revolved. Master and Mistress Spendlove had not raised Samson Lyle. Yet the task had been owned by parents who were as distant from each other as they were to their young son. They had money, the Lyles, a modest acorn of inheritance nurtured into a formidable oak by guile in the mercantile world, which ensured comfort at home that precious few could rival, especially when the first of the wars began. But his parents' match had been one made by others. A marriage of convenience that would forge alliances and oversee transactions but utterly inconvenient for those whose lives it would affect. Young Samson knew from almost the moment he could walk. A coldness between his mother and father. An estrangement in mind if not in body that was the hallmark of their union, a wedge driven between them, first by bitterness, then later by wine.

Thus, his modest, erudite and kind schoolmaster had stepped, unknowingly at first, into the breach. He had taught Lyle in a scholarly fashion, of course but also in life's intangibles. How to conduct oneself in polite company. How to treat others with respect and kindness. How to stand tall and defend a principle. Ursula Spendlove had made her own mark in Lyle's life, showing a young, impetuous man patience and empathy. She and her husband had demonstrated, in their quiet, unassuming manner, how successful a marriage could be and Lyle, when the time came, had modelled his own upon theirs. In so many ways the Spendloves had had a formative influence on Samson Lyle. Ultimately, he had to save Botolph, because he could not let them down. Could not disappoint Ursula's memory.

"Botolph is like a brother to me," Lyle said, dragging his thoughts from the hapless lad's parents, "though he knows it not."

"Well he ain't no brother to me," Grumm muttered.

"And that is why you are free to turn Tyrannus around if it please you."

"Good," Grumm grunted, patting his horse's neck appreciatively. "Then I shall."

They rode on in silence. The bridleway climbed a steep slope for a hundred yards, its leaf-littered banks diminishing. As it reached ground level, distant hilltops visible like dark etchings through the trees, it opened onto a broad fair-meadow of long grass that shifted with the vagaries of the wind. A nye of pheasants exploded from cover at the appearance of the riders, feathers flying as a half-dozen screeching birds scattered pell-mell in panic, while a small roe deer meandered further off, apparently untroubled as it tore up wads of grass and absently skirted patches of vicious-looking gorse. Thick stands of thistles marked a track across the field, flanking the hoof-worn route like a malevolent avenue. With their dark leaves and razor spikes, they were miniature pike-blocks to Lyle's eye and his mind wandered like the fawn, transporting him to other, distant fields, gore-spattered and smoke-wreathed. He had been blooded, the teenaged Lyle, at the decisive Battle of Naseby but the conflict had not ended there. Parliament's remodelled and formidable new army, with Lyle in its ranks, had barely paused for breath when they had been dispatched to deal with Royalists in Wales. Then it had been riots back in England, more Cavalier resistance in Kent and a new threat from the north as the Scots Engagers had crossed the border having made an alliance with the imprisoned monarch. There followed Preston and Winwick Pass, clashes of arms that had simultaneously annihilated the Engagers, ended the Second Civil War and made a man out of Samson Lyle. He could still smell those battles. Still hear them. Yet nothing could have prepared him for Ireland. The beginning of the end of his old life.

He had been a war hero by then. A dashing, deadly major in the formidable cavalry of the all-conquering Army of Parliament, sent to quell resistance across the sea. Except that war in Ireland was different. It was more brutal. Crueller. A conflict fuelled by hatred rather than principle. Finally came Limerick, where Lyle had seen and done things that had brought him such horror, such remorse, that he had thought he might drown in his own shame. He had turned his back. Ridden Star hard to the sea and then on to England. Ireton, his friend and master, had dispatched troops to intercept him and, somehow, they had reached Lyle's home first. He had arrived to discover that she was already dead. Alice; how he missed her. She was long gone. She was bones. A memory. Yet not a single hour slipped by without her haunting him.

"What's the bliddy plan, then, you mad bastard?" Eustace Grumm's coarse voice grated across his bow.

Lyle blinked hard, forcing pin-pricks from his eyes and images from his head. He smiled at the Cornishman. "We find Marek's missing book and give it back."

Grumm sniffed. "He's probably offed the boy regardless."

"No, he wants his property. Botolph is surety. It makes no sense to kill him." In the distance a thick pall of smoke belched from what was probably a charcoal-maker's ferocious fire. He watched it gather above the trees. "Not yet, leastwise."

"Well then," Grumm replied with mock primness, "that's all tied up in a nice neat bow. We search the countryside for a special little book and just hand it back to Marek. No trouble."

Lyle laughed. "Ye of little faith, Eustace."

"Well forgive my sceptical heart, Samson Lyle but how in bastard blazes are we going to find the damnable thing?"

"We'll find it, old friend," Lyle answered, "because I know who really took it."

*

East Meon, Hampshire

The loud rap at the door echoed the length of the huge hall, forcing Colonel Francis Maddocks to look up from the thick stack of papers that had found their way to his table seemingly moments after sunup. With an irritable grunt he sat back in the chair, its polished stanchions creaking under his muscular frame and pushed the piled communiques away. "Come!"

His hair, raven black but shot through with silver flecks, fell loose about his shoulders. He quickly swept the strands away from his face as the young, mud-spattered soldier strode into the grand chamber on loping legs that were stick-thin and disproportionately long. Maddocks raised a single brow. "To what do I owe this dubious pleasure, Lieutenant Grimes?" He stood, moving away from the enormous hunk of oak and crossing the line of intricately patterned turkey carpets that had been laid out on his arrival. He reached the nearest window, a large rectangle of diamond panes and stared out at brooding skies that had dumped so much rain upon the outbuildings, orchards, forests and hills. The road that ran adjacent to the hall was empty still. In an hour or two it would be a morass. He turned to look quizzically at Grimes. "It is no easy ride from Petersfield in this weather. You must have departed before the sun."

Grimes, lobster-tailed helm wedged in the crook of his arm, bowed low, a particular effort for his willowy frame and, noticing watery filth forming a puddle about his tall boots, danced a brisk sidestep to put himself clear of the plush rug. The movement, all legs and arms, put Maddocks in mind of a giant crab scuttling across a rock. Grimes was a sallow specimen, with lower eyelids that exposed red-raw flesh where they drooped but his hazel eyes glistened with awe as they roamed the hall. "I was woken by word of a fracas, sir."

"Splendid, is it not?" Maddocks said, noting the lieutenant's interest. "When touring Major-General Goffe's territory, I am ever thankful to reach this place." He laughed as an image of his townhouse overlooking Petersfield marketplace pushed itself to the fore. "Tis more befitting of a man of my dignity than a view over cattle pens."

"It is like a fortress, sir," Grimes answered, still marvelling, "with walls so stout."

"Malmstone and flint," said Maddocks, "four feet thick." He could understand the younger man's wonder, for in a village of timber and thatch, the ancient complex of Court Hall was as unusual as it was intimidating.

Grimes's mouth twisted in evident distaste. “An old bishop's lair, so they say.”

Maddocks nodded. “The Bishops of Winchester, no less. Maintained as a home and as a court house too. Praise God, such trappings were stripped from those ne’er-do-wells when their posts were abolished.” He spread his own gaze appreciatively about the room. The hall itself, a throwback to times long faded, was almost fifty feet long, he reckoned and near thirty wide. The high, cavernous ceiling of black beams held up a magnificent louvred roof of many thousands of tiles and the glowing hearth could have accommodated an entire boar for the spit. Major-General William Goffe governed the region on behalf of the Lord Protector but it was his hand-picked commissioners and their military facilitators that did the real work. To the likes of Maddocks fell the enforcement of law and the reformation of public morality. Gambling dens, playhouses and baiting pits were to be suppressed. Public gatherings were to be broken up, old Royalists kept at bay, seditious activity crushed. Drunkenness, sexual licentiousness, foul-language and blasphemy were all to be severely punished, while alehouses known for clientele of an unruly nature could expect to be closed. And all that fell upon Maddocks's shoulders in the eastern and southern parts of the County of Southampton. To that end, he was compelled to travel, almost like a monarch of old, embarked upon perpetual progress. He had a dozen regular rest stops and of those, this was by far his favourite. If only it were his permanent residence, he thought ruefully but that privilege had been bestowed upon one of the Army grandees who had come out of the late war with gold-lined pockets and the ear of the Protector. The only condition to snapping up the manor at auction for a veritable steal was that the old bishop's court would be made available whenever it was requested by the new regime. "Now then," he said, clapping his hands. "This fracas."

Lieutenant Grimes scratched a chin crammed with white-headed pimples. He sniffed wetly. "Up in the hills, at Chalton. The Red Lion."

Maddocks knew the place and waved a dismissive hand. "Drunks comparing pizzles, no doubt."

The lieutenant licked thin lips nervously. "I fear it was a deal more serious than that, sir."

"Anyone die?"

"No, sir but there was some trouble with a parcel of foreign sell-swords, led by a fellow named Marek."

That gave Maddocks pause. He felt his features tighten, though he fought to remain impassive. "Mercenaries?" he said incredulously. "In Southamptonshire? What were they about; doing battle with sheep?"

"A lad was beaten," Grimes answered.

"Not badly, Mister Grimes, or he would not have dragged himself all the way to your door."

Grimes shook his head, though the brown hair plastered to his forehead by sweat and mud did not shift. "It was not reported by the victim, sir. They drank the inn quite dry, these sell-swords. The tapster was forced to travel to town in order to replenish his ale."

"And he took the opportunity to lodge his complaint with you." Maddocks stared out of the window. The muffled sound of a watermill cranked and thudded outside. "Foreign mercenaries," he muttered, considering the assertion. "Man by the name of Marek. I wonder."

"He is known to you, sir?"

"Perhaps. Not mercenaries, Grimes," Maddocks said, for it just did not ring true. The old sovereign's three kingdoms had been infested with rough, godless killers during the civil wars.

Men who had crossed from the conflict in the Low Countries when coins and enemies had begun to run dry. But those days had long faded. The creation of Parliament's New Modelled Army had initially stifled the need for such men. "Our final victory," he said aloud, "has ensured a peace that shall, God willing, last until Jesus' return." He snapped his fingers. "Not soldiers, Grimes but sailors. Pirates in all but name. Blake's squadron are in. The lawless knaves in his employ are worse than Barbary corsairs. General Goffe has petitioned the Protector on the matter, on account of the propensity of those same villains to roam his jurisdiction betwixt London and Portsmouth. Heathens in the main. Irish and French, Musselmen, pagan and Papist." He strode back to the desk, plucking a small, pale-green pod from a pouch that lay beside the papers. He offered it up. "Cardamom?" When Grimes politely demurred, Maddocks took a second to split open the thin outer shell with a well-practised thumb, tilted back his head and upended it into his mouth. A cascade of tiny seeds scattered his tongue and he chewed vigorously. "Restores the breath," he explained when Grimes stared in evident bewilderment. "In short, we have a pure Army and a rotten Navy. That's your answer. But what concern is it of mine? I would not readily interfere with Blake's crews on account of a mere brabble in a tippling house."

"He was abducted, sir."

"The Chalton lad? The one they beat?" Maddocks grunted. "Condemned with shapely legs, was he? Months at sea and all that." He smothered his own mirth when he read only unease on his subordinate's face. After all, the lad had not ridden from Petersfield to share a jest. "Presumably you have dealt with this matter yourself, man?" He paused as a troop of horsemen, clad head-to-toe in leather and metal, thundered past the window to draw up outside Court Hall. When the thrum of their hoof-beats had ebbed, Maddocks continued, "Did you not make direct for Chalton?"

"I did, sir. The miscreants had already departed."

"They will be travelling down to Portsmouth," Maddocks said. "Hardly a pebble in a dung heap. Ride the lanes. Track them down, bring them in and free the bloody boy." Again, Grimes's expression struck a note of disquiet and Maddocks began to lose patience. "Lieutenant," he snapped, "speak plain. What the devil is this about?"

"The Ironside Highwayman," Grimes said pointedly, "was present at the Red Lion. Almost came to blows with the foreign ruffians."

Maddocks could not keep his features impassive this time, his brow screwing unbidden into a dark frown. "Indeed? You're certain?"

"Tavern-keeper told me so, sir. By his account, the sailors accused the Chalton boy of stealing something from them. Something precious. The Ironside Highwayman was supping therein and took it upon himself to intervene."

"He would not easily pick such men as enemies. The thief must have been a member of his sordid little gang." Maddocks knitted his fingers across his stomach. "Tell me they ran the blackguard through. Lord above but it would save me a deal of trouble."

"Alas, no," Grimes replied.

"Then?"

"There was something of a standoff, sir. Concluding only when the bandit pledged to recover the missing item."

They were interrupted by a thump at the massive, iron-clasped doors. "Come!" Maddocks barked. The door opened and a servant ushered another soldier inside. He was a middle-aged man with close-cropped auburn hair, a broken nose and neat, white teeth. Maddocks acknowledged the man who had ridden at the head of the newly arrived group of cavalrymen with a curt nod. "Major Smith. Welcome. My man will bring refreshment forthwith." The major, as muddy and travel-worn as the lieutenant but devoid of the junior officer's temerity, gave his thanks and walked directly to the far end of the hall and the hearth's warming embrace. Already he was plucking off his leather gloves and shrugging his way out of the saffron coloured scarf – the mark of Colonel Maddocks' Regiment of Horse – that swathed his torso.

Maddocks turned back to Grimes. "This precious item. The Highwayman has it?"

Grimes shook his head. "He claimed not, sir but this Marek declined to believe him."

"Of course he declined," Maddocks gave a snort of amusement. "A weasel like Samson Lyle would not risk his skin for a stranger. You are aware of his treachery, yes?"

"Was a major," Grimes said, "in the Parliament's remodelled army. Fought to great acclaim, so I heard. A friend to General Ireton and," his voice took on a note of dread as he spoke the names, "even, they say, to the Lord Protector himself."

Maddocks nodded, unable to keep the sourness from his face or tone. "And to me, more's the pity. But he lost his nerve. When King Jesus called for warriors in Ireland, Lyle's ears were deaf. His pride and his cowardice condemned him to turn his coat and then his tail."

"They say his goodwife was killed," Grimes ventured tentatively.

"A mishap." Maddocks shrugged. "A tragedy, without doubt but not intentional. Troopers were dispatched to his home. Goodwife Lyle behaved rather rashly and was injured by one of the horses. If blame is to be apportioned, let it befall Lyle himself, whose treason brought about all. Now the Almighty sees fit for the knave to wander the roads with a price around his neck. Eventually, God willing, the price will be replaced by a noose." He hooked a thumb into his breeches. "Chalton, then. What was taken?"

"Treasure, sir and a book of some kind. The tapster knew only that."

Maddocks sighed heavily, not wishing to leave the comforts of East Meon prematurely. "I suppose I should investigate this business myself. Thank you, Lieutenant Grimes. You were right to inform me." He pressed the balls of his hands into stinging eyes. "Outlaws, pirates and treasure in our sleepy hills, eh? Whatever next?"

From the fireplace, a deep voice intoned, "You've heard the madman's rant too, Colonel? A good tale spreads on the wind, I do declare!"

Both Maddocks and Grimes looked to the medieval hall's far end. "Major Smith?" the colonel prompted.

"The madman," Smith said in jovial fashion, his palms held flat towards the heat. "Deserter, taken by my lads at Havant. Red-handed, no less, in the act of stealing parchment."

"What of it?"

"We found a deal of booty in his possession. Treasure, of sorts, that he claims he stole from pirates!" Smith brayed with laughter. "He's a talented storyteller, I'll give him that. A shame he'll soon swing for his crimes."

Maddocks turned back to the lieutenant. "Mister Grimes, rouse the men, if you please." He left the table and went to a low chest, upon which his sword and scabbard lay. Collecting them up, he added, "And fetch my horse."

*

Finchdean, Hampshire

Lyle had only Amelia for company when Star loped towards the hamlet nestled deep in the wooded hills. Misty fingers lingered stubbornly on the highest slopes, writhing over the treetops as the half-hearted breeze worked to push them clear.

"What happened to him?" Amelia asked as they came off the last hill and followed the line of a hawthorn hedge towards the clustered thatches.

Lyle felt her weight shift to the side and realised she was inspecting Star's coat. "Exploding gun at Worcester Fight."

She traced the patch of pink, mutilated skin that blighted the beast's flank. "Must have been a big gun."

Lyle nodded. "A scrap of iron near cut him in twain."

She straightened again. "I do not remember the war."

"Then you are fortunate."

"Bella told me about what happened." She hesitated, then ventured in a small voice, "To your wife, I mean."

"Bella has a big mouth."

"I… cannot imagine…"

"No," Lyle said curtly, "you cannot." He immediately regretted his tone, adding, "It is why my war continues." The addendum had been designed to offer some explanation, as if the information would go some way to softening his brusqueness but all it did was invite the memory of Marek's scornful words and they crowded in, like birds descending upon a new-sown field. *He may dress like a cavalry officer but that does not make him one.* Did the jibe ring true? Had he become, in truth, no different than a common footpad? No different than Whistler? He glanced down at the accoutrements of a warrior. The sword and the pistol. The dagger and the hammer. Baubles now. Used occasionally and then mostly for threat above substance.

"You fight to honour her," Amelia said. "To punish them for taking her from you."

"Aye," Lyle replied, his voice thickening with a sudden pang of loss.

"And to remind yourself of who you were," she added. "And are still."

Her understanding took him by surprise and all he could do was offer a dumb nod. He fought for Alice, certainly but also in a desperate attempt to piece together the fractured shards of his old self. The identity to which he still clung like a drowning man upon a disintegrating spar. Without the Ironside Highwayman, there was nothing left of Samson Lyle. Just a ghost in a long cloak.

"Your reasons matter not to me," Amelia was saying, perhaps sensing his sudden unease. "You risk your life for Botolph and I am indebted."

"He is yet in danger," Lyle said as they moved beyond the hedgerow and onto the gravel track that led into the village proper. The surrounding fields were busy already with labourers and livestock but here, in the valley, Finchdean was almost silent. Smoke trails meandered from the rooftops, a pair of buzzards circled lazily far above but there was little beyond the lowing of distant cattle to greet them.

"And not only my brother," she said sorrowfully. "My father is an old man."

"Your father was the logical choice."

"What if they catch sight of him?"

"They will not *lose* sight of him, Miss Spendlove," he answered, amused that she would imagine her elderly father and his lumbering pony and trap could hope to follow a band of seasoned fighting men through the countryside undetected. "But they'll pay him no heed."

"I pray you are right."

They reached the triangular patch of turf at the village's heart. A tavern's painted sign creaked as it swayed gently on rusted hinges and the occasional clang and murmur came from behind the brick walls of a smithy.

"Ho, Ned!" Lyle called as Star crossed the green, slowing so that he could tear up wads of grass. At the farthest side was a hunched figure dressed in tattered breeches and a poor man's coat that would offer scant comfort against the cold. He was seated on a low bench, legs outstretched. He gradually stirred at the words, lifting his face to squint blearily at the newcomers. Lyle spoke again, "And how fare you this bright morning?"

"Major?" the man murmured softly. He was in his early thirties, with a dense thicket of brown hair, broad shoulders and a pulpy complexion. He shifted his rump, face creasing in an agonised wince. His legs only moved a fraction, accompanied by the clank of iron.

Lyle slid down from the horse, offering a hand to Amelia. As she moved, his nostrils were full of the scent of her hair and it was all he could do not to lean in. Clearing his throat awkwardly, he plucked an earthenware bottle from a saddlebag and inspected the stocks in which Ned's ankles had been fastened. His feet were naked and caked in grime. "How long have you been here?"

"A day and two nights, thus far." Ned hawked up a gobbet of frothy spittle and deposited it on the grass.

Amelia's face was a mask of pity. "What was your crime, sir?"

"Imbibed a cup or two." Ned gave a rueful grunt. "Or ten."

Lyle looked up and around. At Finchdean's doors and windows, into the mouth of every lane and up at the sheep-dotted fields. "Commissioner's men?"

Ned spat again. "Locked me up and sauntered off, God afflict them with plague. I'm to be released at noon, so they say but I shall not hold my breath for it."

Lyle nodded sympathetically. The intimation was that the

local lawmen could do what they damned-well pleased and Ned was probably right. After the Instrument of Government had made Cromwell Lord Protector, he had divided the nation into regions that would be governed by his trusted major-generals. Assisted by their specially appointed commissioners and bolstered by an all-powerful army, the generals and their aides were effectively untouchable. "I will fetch my war-hammer."

"No, Major, do not," Ned warned. "I cannot be seen to gain freedom by such means. I'll find myself back here in a trice, with my sentence doubled."

Lyle sucked his teeth with irritation but eventually acquiesced. "I would speak with you, all the same."

"Jesu, man, do not be foolish," Ned said, palming his eyes. When he met Lyle's gaze again, his own was sharper than before. "Nowhere is safe. Get away before you are seen." He glanced across at the blacksmith's forge. "They'll open up soon. And Goody Pring will throw back the tavern's shutters in short order. They're honest folk, hereabouts but they'll sell you down the river for that plump reward."

Lyle crouched beside Ned. "I will not tarry long."

Ned's expression tightened. "Jesu, Major, pay heed. The Mad Ox has agents everywhere."

"The Mad Ox has chased me for many months without success."

Ned glanced up at the tavern's shuttered first floor. "He pays them well for information. They will see-"

"They will see a kindly Samaritan," Lyle cut him off, lifting the bottle, "offering water to slake a man's thirst. Let them report such a tale to their superiors. The constable has gone, you say. Well, are there soldiers hereabouts? Mounted men?"

"No," Ned conceded.

"Then let his spies watch." He handed Ned the drink. "Here."

When the fettered man had quaffed the water as though it

were the very elixir of youth, sleeving his mouth and passing back the bottle, he said, "God bless you, Major, truly. But how did you know to find me here?"

"Here or the taphouse, old friend."

"The village drunk, you mean to say," Ned said, with a sideways glance of sheer embarrassment at Amelia. When Lyle did not respond, Ned sighed deeply, sadly, then asked, "What, then, of your friends? How fares that sharp-tongued stripling?"

"Bella is well."

"And your smuggler? Old goat dead yet?"

Lyle laughed. "Not when last I checked." And he prayed that was still true. He had dispatched them both to the south. Grumm to the next village on the road, Rowlands Castle and Bella all the way to Havant. There to ask questions.

"I am glad. And this young lady?" Ned looked pointedly at Amelia.

"The less said, the better for all," Lyle replied. "In truth, my presence at your beleaguered side is not entirely selfless."

Ned grimaced. "I cannot help, Major. I served you in the wars and I'm proud of that. But it is too fraught." He gave a bleak chuckle. "Look at me. This is what befalls a man who indulges in strong drink. What awaits he who treats with outlaws?"

Lyle could hardly blame his old comrade. That was why he had come prepared. He leaned forwards, placing the bottle on the grass beneath the bench. "Do not discard this, Ned. Drink the rest, take it home," he winked, "and throw it at a wall."

Ned glanced down at the bottle, then back to Lyle. After a moment's hesitation, "What do you need?"

"A thief may have come through here. A man I encountered first at Idsworth chapel. I have need of him." Lyle cast his mind back to the rain-soaked encounter beneath the solitary beech. "Said he was Portsmouth bound. If he spoke true, that places him on the Finchdean road, south, then on through Rowlands castle and Havant."

Ned's brow furrowed in consideration. "Name?"

"Whistler, he called himself. An old soldier, in fact. A malignant. Though this one deserted at Cheriton Fight. Earned a branded hand for his trouble."

"What's he done, this malignant?"

"Better that you steer a wide berth, Ned. But have you seen him? If anyone witnessed him pass through the village," he shrugged, apologetic for the statement, "it is surely the man who cannot leave."

It was a cruel thing to say, he supposed but truthful nevertheless. How far this man, this ragged sot, had fallen since riding to war on a noble destrier. It made him think of his words to Wardley Spendlove. There but for the Grace of God. How close had Lyle come to following Ned to the bottom of a wine cask after Alice had died? In the end, it had been the sword and the challenge of the duel that had brought him back from the brink. The time he had spent in French exile, the hours he had wiled in the school of Charles Besnard, absorbing the great master's knowledge. The more he had learned, the less his grief had hurt but it could all have been so different. Privately he shuddered.

To Lyle's relief, Ned laughed, this time with real mirth. "I seen many folk, sir. Pilgrims and traders. Children mostly. The little rats love to whip off my shoes and taunt my toes with feathers. I seen mariners too. A dozen or thereabouts. Fiendish looking buggers. Paid little heed to me and for that I was thankful. Haven't spied a motley company like that since before Worcester."

Lyle shared a look with Amelia. "Where are they now?"

Ned jutted his chin in a southerly direction. "Goody Pring wouldn't serve their like, so full are they of lice and pox. They've gone to find a steading with its own brewhouse. Plenty about."

"Did they have a prisoner with them? A young lad?"

"Not that I noticed. Mind you, they had a cart and nag. What I took to be a wounded comrade lying in back."

"Wounded, certainly," Lyle replied, "but no comrade." So Marek had been good to his word. They were travelling to the docks as planned. How close had they passed to the true object of their ire, he wondered, though they would not have known it? He pressed, "But not a lone stranger?"

Ned shook his head. "Regrettably, Major."

"Are you certain, old friend? A scrawny man, twitching and nervous, fingers missing on one hand and a deserter's brand upon the other. You saw no such fellow?"

Ned screwed up his face in apology. "Not a hide nor hair."

*

Rowlands Castle, Hampshire

By the time Lyle and Amelia had completed the two mile stretch down to Rowlands Castle, the day had begun in earnest. All trace of mist had gone, eradicated by a low-slung, dazzling sun and replaced in patches by vapour trails wafting from the mouths of folk about their business. The skies were no longer so brooding, which seemed to animate the carters and their whinnying palfreys, thundering back and forth along the ancient high road about which two-score homes, a chapel, a stinking tannery, cavernous warehouses and many more had grown. It was a small enough place, named for a Norman fort that had long since crumbled but, like Petersfield to the north and Havant to the south, the streets were well-maintained and the newer buildings mostly brick and tile, a sign of the prosperity brought by local fleeces that were unsurpassed for quality.

Lyle angled his hat to obscure his face as Star loped casually into the midst of the village. He had hidden his distinctive war-hammer and double-barrelled pistol in his saddlebags, though eyes were naturally drawn to the long sword at his hip and the woman with immodestly unbound hair riding pillion. He checked and rechecked the road behind, routes to the flanks and any other means of rapid departure, should such recourse become necessary. A gang of small children crossed the street ahead, scuttling like a gaggle of noisy geese towards a handsome, two-storied house of thick chimney stacks and mullioned windows. A petty school, he supposed and he wondered how education might have changed since Cromwell's rise. No more the endless recitals of kings and queens that he had been subjected to. No more High Church prayer book or the ingrained sense of fealty to prince or bishop. The brave new world left no part of society untouched.

He spotted Eustace Grumm, on foot and holding Tyrannus's bridle in a gloved fist, at the front of a bakery. He steered Star over to where the Cornishman waited. "What news?"

"Nowt," Grumm replied with a wet sniff. "And no sign of your pirates. What did you discover?"

"Hood," Lyle prompted.

Grumm's white eyebrows pressed together. "I am not known here, Major."

"When abroad, you conceal your identity," Lyle said. "That was the agreement."

Grumm blew a jet of air through his red nose but raised the hood all the same. Though Lyle was a well-known figure in the area, flirting with discovery always, his associates carried no such burden. When not assisting the Ironside Highwayman, Eustace Grumm played the part of John Brown, tapster at the Red Lion in Rake. Bella assumed the role of Lucy, his niece and together they were afforded a degree of normality. As long as they were never spied in the company of the notorious Samson Lyle. “Very well,” Grumm muttered. “May I learn what you have learned, or must I guess?”

“We did not locate Whistler. He has vanished, it seems.”

“Slippery little bastard,” Grumm spat.

Lyle raised an eyebrow at that. “My, how you've changed.” Eustace Grumm had been chief of a smuggling ring in his native Cornwall. All manner of dark deeds had been the hallmarks of his illicit trade in the perpetual struggle with rival gangs and Customs Men alike. But after the latter enemy had been tipped-off as to his whereabouts one summer's evening in the uneasy and short-lived truce following the First Civil War, he had barely escaped England with his skin intact. The following years of exile and destitution had not been kind, culminating in a fateful run-in with thief-takers in a Parisian tavern and an impromptu meeting with a high branch and a makeshift noose. As fate or providence would have it, Samson Lyle, himself a landless, lawless traveller, had been supping in that same tavern. He had stepped into the argument like an avenging angel, with his soldierly manner and assortment of strange weapons and Grumm had been plucked from death's clutches. They had ridden together ever since, though that did not prevent Lyle from chiding his comrade when the mood took hold.

Grumm screwed up his face. “What I did,” he answered sourly, “I did to survive. And you're hardly at liberty to deride, infamous outlaw that you be.”

Lyle laughed. “Touché.”

“Now tell me. Did you see the sailors?”

“They're near Finchdean,” Lyle said.

“And the boy?” The Cornishman’s wrinkled face tightened a fraction as he glanced at Amelia. “Young Botolph.”

Lyle felt her move in the saddle and hoped she was acknowledging Grumm’s inferred apology. He shrugged. “We must presume so."

Grumm made a clacking sound with his tongue. "Not in any haste, are they?"

"Their ship is not yet due for departure. And they're hardly concerned with alluding us. If anything, it serves Marek's purpose to remain visible, lest I produce the book."

"Must think you a miracle worker," Grumm said sourly. "What of the authorities? Surely Maddocks or his underlings have received word of these braggartly bastards? Traipsing cross country like blood-thirsty Landsknechts, kidnapping locals where they may. The Army cannot sit back and ignore such doings."

"*If* he has received word," replied Lyle, "then he'll be reluctant to intervene. These are Robert Blake's men and Blake is Cromwell's personal ban-dog against the Spanish. He has the Protector's favour."

"They're Papists!"

"They're experienced hands to a man."

"Ergo, they are above the law?"

Lyle nodded. "And they know it."

"What of Botolph?" Grumm asked. "They cannot simply swagger into Portsmouth with a youngster trussed up like a Christ-tide goose!"

"We are at war with the Spanish, Eustace. Any man-o'-war's crew may use impressment to bolster their complement."

Grumm pursed his cracked lips as understanding dawned. "And that's what the buggers'll claim they're about."

"The navy needs hands and the Protector needs victories. Maddocks would not lift a finger, even if he had a mind to. Marek will take his time, sample the local ales and wander down to his ship with Botolph Spendlove at his mercy. When the missing treasure does not find its way into his hands, the *Diamond* will set sail and Botolph will be doomed."

Grumm blasphemed softly, tugging the matted strands of his beard in frustration. “So it is down to us.”

“And we cannot free Botolph without possessing either a small army or Marek’s book.”

“Which we do not have. And we cannot get it because we do not know where the real thief's bliddy-well at.”

“Oh yes we do!” the words of a girl severed their discussion. Lyle turned, startled, in his saddle and Grumm looked up sharply, because the voice was coarser, brasher and pitched higher than Amelia’s. The rider, grinning widely, brought her mare, Newt, to a fidgety standstill and offered a bow from the waist.

“Bella?” Lyle said.

“That whistling fellow,” she answered. “I’ve found him!”

*

Warblington Castle, Hampshire

The prisoner was bound so tightly at the wrists that his skin bled. He could hear the guard’s approach long before he saw him, for the jangle of keys at the man’s belt was like a herald’s trumpet in the silence.

He braced himself, screwing shut his good eye against the flood of light. He hissed aloud, jolted by the pain of the other eye that had been reduced to a blackened, puffy mess by a soldier’s gauntleted knuckles.

He had been sitting against the damp brickwork of the cell wall when the iron-bound door juddered open but rose almost miraculously to his feet, his weight hauled without effort by rough hands at the scruff of his neck. He could not see the man who had dragged him upright, for the searing light cast the fellow in shadow but the familiar odour of onions and salted fish did the job of identification well enough.

"Where do you take me, Hobb?" Whistler blurted as his feet scrabbled in the soiled rushes, failing to keep pace with his body.

The prison guard, a squat, strongly built Kentishman, limped awkwardly as he spoke. "Colonel's here."

"Colonel?" Whistler echoed as they went through the doorway and out into the crisp noon air. He stole a look behind, finally getting to see in daylight the place where he had been incarcerated under the cover of night. It was a plain, single-storied barn, built in stone, with a tiled roof and only a single, high owl-hole for light and ventilation. Christ, he thought but how welcome a cold winter's day could be when one had been deprived of it. He breathed deeply, lungs smarting, as they crossed what he now saw was an expansive yard, the ground a muddy lattice of water-filled wheel-ruts. Outbuildings of various size and purpose fringed the open space, interspersed by great drifts of masonry, as if the rain clouds had contained bricks as well as water.

Hobb, leading the way with his strange waddle and a pungent onion trail, nodded a jowly head towards the far corner of the yard. "In there."

Whistler looked up. High above everything, an octagonal tower loomed, built in fine brick and dressed in grey stone. He knew it had been part of a larger structure once, the adjoining portions of abruptly ending curtain wall told him that much but those high ramparts had long been torn down, the once-formidable home undermined and slighted by a victorious, vengeful army. The tower was a lone feature now, incongruous and isolated above this modest wasteland. "What is that place?"

"Gatehouse turret," Hobb said, adjusting further his awkward gait to account for hidden pitfalls and slimy dung. "Only bit left of the old castle." He glanced back with a lopsided grin.

"Garrisoned by your lot. Smashed up by ours."

Whistler watched a large kite do wheeling battle with a pair of noisy magpies above the crenellations. "My lot," he said bitterly.

The stocky guard grunted in amusement. "Yours forever, now that you bear the king's mark on your flesh."

Whistler stole a rueful glance at his bound hands, one of which would not open fully, for the seared and puckered palm had healed as tight as a drum skin. They had talked briefly, he and Hobb, after his arrival at the tumbledown castle. Hobb had been a Roundhead pikeman, seeing action in the early throes of the war, before the bullet from a harquebusier's carbine had shattered his thigh. It was strange for Whistler to consider the Royalist cause his own, since he had fled those terrifying ranks as soon as the chance had come but he supposed Hobb was right. He still stared at the remnant of what once must have been a magnificent gatehouse. Lower down, he noticed, part of the original arch remained. "Why leave that one turret?"

"Tis a landmark," Hobb answered. "Helps ships navigate Langstone channel." They were nearing the foot of the turret, where a set of time-smoothed steps led the way up to an open doorway. He grinned. "Also makes for a convenient home for miscreants such as yourself."

"Whistler, is it?"

The speaker had to be the colonel that Hobb had mentioned. Of the trio of soldiers lurking in the gloomy, musty-smelling chamber to which Whistler had been conveyed, the colonel was the only man seated. He appeared to be in his early forties, with long, dark hair that was streaked with silver. His broad shoulders filled a fine green coat that was slashed at the sleeves to show a silken lining of rich yellow, while across his chest, right shoulder to left hip, there was wrapped a broad scarf, the colour of saffron, bearing the black insignia of a lion's head.

Whistler made the mistake of meeting the colonel's eye. He wrenched his own eyes away quickly, cowed by the nonchalant disdain in the cool grey gaze. "Aye," he managed to say, though it was an effort to force the words out of a throat suffering sudden drought. The colonel yawned expansively and licked his lips. He was lord of this place, a deadly beast in his lair and Whistler's eyes were drawn inexorably back to the lion. "That... that is to say, Whistler be my name."

The colonel glanced left and right at the other men, flanking the table on either side like a pair of grim sentinels, their faces devilish in the shadows thrown by tremulous candle flame. One was tall and stick thin, the other so portly that his scarf, fastened about his waist with a large knot, looked fit for tearing. The tall man, blighted by a facial tick that never seemed to settle, rubbed his hands together against the cold, putting Whistler in mind of a fly alighting upon meat. He glowered. "Sir."

Whistler nodded frantically. "Sir."

"Do you have a real name?" the fly asked. "A Christian name? What did your mother call you?"

"Never knew her, sir," Whistler replied, achingly aware of the final syllable's absurd trilling. "Was always Whistler, long as I can remember."

"A veritable songbird," the colonel said, then, "My name is Maddocks." On the desk before him was a small chest, a plate bearing a selection of marchpanes that had been cut into wedges and a large silver goblet, which he now lifted to his lips.

Maddocks. The name made Whistler's guts clench. It was all he could do not to fall to his knees and sob into the man's boots. He swallowed hard, forcing back a stinging surge of bile.

Unaware or unconcerned, Colonel Maddocks continued, "I apologise for the crumble-down nature of this place but it will have to serve."

Instinctively, Whistler's eyes roamed. The place in question, he was beginning to realise, had once been a hub of work and governance. The ancient castle's chancery, perhaps, where documents were scribed, sanded and sealed. Besides the table, some of the accoutrements of administration remained, like fragments of memory. A couple of larger chests in the far corners. Shelves still clinging to the wainscoted walls between iron sconces adorned with elaborate oak-sprig motifs. But now the chests were empty, the wainscoting flaky and the sconces rusted. Like the rest of the castle, it was a place of ghosts and former glories, a chamber left to moulder.

As if reading his mind, Maddocks said, "The tower, here, makes for a convenient perch as I fly about the county."

Whistler managed a mute nod. While never claiming to be au fait with the logistical machinations of the Protectorate and its grandees, he knew well enough that Cromwell had devolved regional governance. The affable and talkative Hobb had told him that Colonel Maddocks, on behalf of Major-General Goffe, engaged in an almost perpetual tour of his jurisdiction, like the progress of a medieval king, centring himself on certain appropriate locations from which he might oversee the mechanisms of justice.

Maddocks reached for the tabletop chest, pushing back the polished lid and taking the topmost leaf of what looked like a deep ream of paper. "Now then, sirrah. Let us discuss your predicament."

Feeling all eyes on him, Whistler felt a sudden pang of terror. The fat soldier, ruddy face glimmering with sweat, sidled away from the wall to stand close. Whistler twisted back, hoping to see a recognisable face but Hobb had long since departed. Returning to Maddocks, he blurted, "I told the other men. The officers what took me. I-"

The fat man punched him. Hard, in the guts, so that Whistler folded in half. A thin trail of vomit erupted into his mouth, leaking from the corners of his lips to speckle his breeches and shoes. A strong hand snagged the scruff of his neck and wrenched him upright.

Maddocks, who had not flinched, scanned the paper in his hand, "You were taken at the parchmenter's, yes?"

"Aye, sir," Whistler uttered hoarsely.

"Theft is a very serious felony in the eyes of the Lord." Maddocks glanced up. "Thou shalt not steal. Tis the seventh commandment."

"What choice," Whistler croaked between heaving gasps, "do a man have?"

Maddocks cocked his head to the side, evidently amused. "Do not steal," he said slowly, as if to a dullard. "As choices present themselves, this one is simple enough, no?"

"When the alternative is starvation?"

"When the reward is eternity in paradise." He looked again at the sheet, then placed it back into the chest. Then he selected one of the marchpanes from the plate and crammed half of it into his mouth. "Now. You are a rotten apple, sirrah. A scourge. One lacking the moral fibre to be of any use to a community. In your time you have thieved," the grey eyes flickered to Whistler's hands, "you have deserted and you have trespassed. Lord only knows what other foul deeds will come to light on the day of judgement. You'll know, from your time as a soldier, that when a limb is rotten, the only remedy is the saw." He paused, letting the image hang in the dank air between them. "It must be cut clean away."

Whistler shook his head, frantically, dizzyingly. "No, sir, no, I beg of you-"

"Unless," Maddocks halted him, raising his hand as well as his voice. When all was silent, he took a long moment to eat the rest of the marchpane, licking his lips with a slowness that made

Whistler want to scream, then leaned back, bending to take something from a low drawer by his knees. He raised it up for all to see and placed it gently on the desk. "This somewhat curious item was found in your possession. Enlighten me, sirrah."

Whistler gazed at the book. He had expected to be quizzed on the matter, for it had been in his snapsack when the watchmen and soldiers had seized him but, seeing it now, he was again struck by its beauty. It was a small thing, really. Not a great deal bigger than a man's flattened palm, its typeface so minuscule that it did not have the bulk of other bibles. But it had been crafted by artists. From the elaborate and vibrant illuminations within its fragile, yellowing pages, to the golden casing that had protected it for generations. "I took it off a party of pirates."

Maddocks had been staring at the bible too but now his eyes darted up to meet those of his prisoner. "Pirates?"

"Looked like the foreign killers we used to have during the late rebellion," Whistler said. "Paid to come to these shores for king or Parliament."

"Mercenaries."

Whistler nodded. "Excepting, this company wore curved cutlasses at their hips, so I took them for sailors of some kind."

"Where did you encounter these ruffians?"

"Up at Guildford. Followed them south."

"Because?"

Whistler glanced to the bible and back. "Because I saw that they did not lack for means."

"And you waited for your chance."

"God forgive me, sir but I did. Followed, watched, waited. Finally the moment came. The big farm above the marsh at Petersfield."

"The Grange. I know it."

"They rested." Whistler shrugged. "I snuck in."

"And you took this," Maddocks said and his hand slid across the golden book. "The Vulgate. The Papist bible." He looked at Whistler, though his fingers remained, tracing patterns over the metalwork. "Hardly a safe item with which to be caught, notwithstanding the precious material in which it is encased. A man could find himself mistaken for a Jesuit priest and disembowelled." Now he let go of the book and propped both elbows on the table, steepling his hands beneath his chin. His glare was hard and unrelenting. "Are you, in fact, an agent of Rome, posted to these Protestant shores by Satan's own Society of Jesus? Did not you hear word of the Lord Protector's recent proclamation? That popish priests be hounded and prosecuted with the full force of the law? That those who say masses and seduce people to the Church of Rome will be speedily and unmercifully convicted?"

"N… N... no, sir," Whistler stuttered, so taken aback was he by the accusation. He felt icy tentacles wrap themselves about his torso as his bowels turned to water and his heart threatened to pound his ribs to dust. "I... I did not know. I cannot even read!"

Maddocks pressed a forefinger against his lips. "Hush, Master Whistler. Hush now, there's a good fellow." He exchanged a smirk with the fat man and the fly. "Even the Jesuits have standards." As the others chuckled and Whistler came near to fainting, Maddocks picked up the bible, turning it in his hands. "So you stole this shiny bauble, not knowing what was within the pages. Blinkered by avarice, you saw only the gold."

"Aye, sir. I had planned to sell it at Portsmouth. Or have the gold stripped."

"But you never reached Portsmouth, on account of your greed."

"On account of my hunger, sir." Whistler felt his gaze slip, unbidden, to the plate of marchpanes.

Maddocks snorted derisively. “You are a villain and you will be dealt with as such. Next market day at Petersfield will suffice. They have room for one more at Gallows Field.”

The fly moved in, rubbing his hands together gleefully, while his portly compatriot took hold of Whistler again. Into Whistler's ear, one of them snarled, “The noose awaits you, lad!” and he bucked and writhed in their implacable grasp but to no avail. They dragged him towards the door, his heels scraping and bouncing along the floor's shattered tiles and he began to weep.

Colonel Francis Maddocks waited for the rumpus to die down before returning his attention to the book.

“Exquisite, Captain Beck, is it not?”

The barrel-like physique of his subordinate filled the doorway. The man, sweating even more profusely than before, wiped chubby hands on his scarf as if to purge them of the prisoner's residue. He frowned at the bible in apparent distaste. “A Romish trinket, sir.”

Maddocks sighed. “One can despise the derivation of an object, John, without despising the object itself.”

“If you say so, sir,” Beck answered primly as he scratched his back against the wall, like a pig at a post.

“I do.” Maddocks handled the book gently, reverently, knowing that his reformist officers would disapprove and not caring one jot. “Yes, I do.”

Beck, as disparaging of Papist ornamentation as he was, appraised the object with a glint in his eye. “Golden filigree?”

Maddocks nodded. “Dominated by an image of the living Christ,” he said, quietly now, unable to hide his awe, “triumphant before the cross.” He ran a finger along the delicate patterns, some of which were inlaid with material the colour of oyster pearls. With his nail he followed each golden thread, caressing them as they swirled. "Around the edges, here, the goldsmith has set red garnets. And here," he indicated the space immediately beneath the cross, "you see these figures? Mourners, on Calvary. The Virgin among them. Such work, John." He breathed out slowly, savouring the moment. "To touch such work." He looked up sharply. "You've heard of Marek Nowak?"

The question clearly wrong-footed Beck, for the captain's mouth flapped silently for a moment or two. Then he shook his head. "I do not believe so, sir."

Lieutenant Grimes, stooping under the lintel, re-entered the room. "Nor I, sir."

Maddocks held up the golden bible. "Its previous owner."

"You know him, sir?" Beck asked, taken aback.

"*Of* him. He has something of a reputation."

"How so?"

Maddocks had studied the bible extensively since arriving in Warblington. The commanding officer of the Havant patrol, a pompous prig by the name of Delaney, had handled the gold-bound object at arm's length, as if the very stench of Beelzebub wafted in its wake. But if Delaney had been only too pleased to be rid of the Papist scriptures, Maddocks had been equally happy to receive them. He knew a valuable trinket when he saw one, even if it did contain the Latin poison that Protestant England spent so much time and energy attempting to eradicate. This wondrous thing had struck him like a heavenly epiphany the moment he had clapped eyes on its ornate cover and he had found himself scrutinising every pattern, every jewel and every page for allegories, maker's marks and any feature of note. "The letters 'MN'," he said, "written just inside." He laid the book on the table, beckoning the others to advance and opened the gold cover to reveal the first page. The initials, inked by hand, were set above the rough sketch of a bird of prey, wings splayed, talons bared. "See the crown atop its head? This is a Polish eagle, gentlemen."

"The pirate?" Grimes asked, reflecting on the prisoner's words.

"The same," Maddocks said. "Except that there are no pirates strolling through Hampshire. There are often, however, plenty of other kinds of mariner. Those who fight the Commonwealth's wars at sea. Shipwrights, caulkers, sailmakers. They walk the lanes between London and Portsmouth." He stabbed the handwritten initials with a forefinger. "There are not many foreign crews in the Commonwealth Navy. Fewer still boasting notorious Polish gun captains. The ship *Diamond* is one such vessel. Marek Nowak is one such gun captain." He sat back. "A fearsome rogue, if ever there was one. As lethal in the prize-fight as he is in battle. You've never heard of him?"

Beck and Grimes shared a nonplussed glance. The former shook his fleshy head. "Should we have, sir?"

"Something of a character amongst Generals at Sea Blake's forces," Maddocks said. "A monster of a pugilist when on land. A divisive figure for his Catholic faith and a fearsome creature for everything else. Fought for his homeland against the Cossacks and Tartars." He paused for a drink, then, clearing his throat, went on, "Survived the Batih massacre, where the Cossacks slaughtered Polish prisoners by the thousand. You'll doubtless recall the horrifying accounts of that atrocity." Invisible feathers played at the skin of his neck as his own memory conjured images he would rather not see. "Days of killing, Captain Beck. To bear witness to such slaughter can only warp the mind." His mouth had dried and he took another sip from the goblet. "After that, enlisted with a Polish merchantman, then found himself sailing under Blake."

Beck wrinkled his flat nose as if he smelled something rotten.

"But a papist, sir. We'd not allow such delinquents to infest the Army."

"The Lord Protector's qualms on that score are not shared by the General at Sea."

"Then why does he not compel Blake?"

"Because Robert Blake wins battles, Captain." Maddocks shrugged. "Winning is everything." He left Beck to splutter indignantly and let his eyes slide back to the treasure. It glowed in the candlelight. Soft and rich and enticing. He smiled. "This is a blessed day, gentlemen. Do you know what this book is?"

"Bible, sir," Grimes offered. "Gold bible, sir."

Maddocks leafed rapidly through the pages of Latin until he reached the back of the text. On the final page there was more handwritten script, though these lines, tiny and faded, had been left by an entirely different scribe. "This is Spanish, gentlemen, which I know neither of you have. But note the date."

Grimes's tall frame leaned over the desk like a willow in a breeze. "1531."

"1531," Maddocks echoed. "1531. The very beginning."

"Beginning, sir?" Grimes said.

"When the heathen Americas began to bleed their vast wealth." He ran his finger over the faint note, silently rereading the words to himself. He looked up at captain and lieutenant in turn. "This bible was owned by a Spaniard. A sailor. He took it across the ocean with Pizarro. I had a suspicion, when first I set eyes on it. But to know the provenance of such a piece is truly breathtaking." Closing and lifting the bible, he rapped his knuckles on the metal bindings. "This is Inca gold, gentlemen. Captured by the conquistadors as they destroyed an entire empire. Some would say it is damned. Cursed, for the blood spilt in its taking. The Spaniards claim it is holy, given them by God for their conquest of a pagan land. Who can tell, truly? But sailors, ever a superstitious breed, revere such baubles as you or

I revere scripture itself. In short, Marek Nowak wants his book back and he'd walk through hell itself to get it. Oh, this really is a blessed day." He laughed when the others simply stared, slack-jawed and lost. "Not only do I have in my possession a priceless treasure but the most ruthless man in the Commonwealth Navy believes the Ironside Highwayman has stolen it. Nowak is not the kind of man to be duped. He and his gun crew are unrepentant papists in a ship full of God-fearing Protestants. They are an aberration in a fleet commanded by reformers. Blake owes his victories at sea to the certain fact that the Almighty is on his side. Yet there Nowak stands, beside his gun, firing hot iron at England's enemies while he counts his rosary and crosses his chest. Nowak is not liked, he is not wanted but he is tolerated. Firstly, because he is good – very good – at the business of killing. Secondly, because he is a man that other men fear. He is not one to be crossed. He is not one to be contradicted. He is not one to be made a fool of. And he believes Samson Lyle has made a fool of him."

Maddocks set the bible down and took another drink as he waited for his words to percolate through his officers' skulls. Captain Beck said, "If we keep the book, sir, this Marek will murder the Chalton fellow."

"An unfortunate consequence, to be certain," Maddocks acknowledged, "but a small sacrifice for the greater good, wouldn't you say?" When he saw Beck was unconvinced, he continued, "Lyle is the worst kind of hypocrite, Captain. A brigand and a traitor, yet brim-full with his own sense of righteousness. He has pledged to retrieve this book. Well, he cannot, for it is here, praise God! But he will yet try to rescue the Chalton man. He won't be able to resist." He looked at Grimes. "And what shall we do, Lieutenant?"

"Nothing, sir?"

"Nothing," Maddocks repeated, satisfied that at least one of his protégés understood the way real life worked. "You and I and Captain Beck, here and all our men will go about our business. We shall return to Petersfield. To Rowlands Castle and to East Meon." He picked up the bible again and opened the little chest. "We shall ride the bridleways, inspect the villages and keep law, order and public morality on behalf of Major-General William Goffe, God bless him. And we shall let Marek Nowak kill the Ironside Highwayman." He placed the bible in the chest and closed the lid. "A fine thing indeed."

*

Portsmouth Point, Portsmouth

The men circled one another like bulldogs in a pit, the fiddler played a jaunty reel, the crowd bayed for blood. The air was thick, hot, infused with spittle and blood, fuggy with the acrid stench of bodies and breath and ale and unadulterated excitement.

Marek Nowak blinked stinging sweat from his eyes, the blurry drape swept quickly away. Across the stained sawdust, panting hard, the twisted features of the leering Turk resolved before him. Like Marek, he was naked from the waist up, broad chest gleaming, the tuft of black hair at his sternum smeared with blood that dripped from his severely buckled nose. There were dark patches at his collarbones and biceps where Marek's attacks had been blocked, leaving bruises that would, God willing, take their own toll as the contest wore on. The Turk's eyes were puffing too, each cut deeply, one at the corner, one right across the lid but within the folds of livid, distended skin the glittering jet stare persisted.

The Jolly Sailor was located to the south of Portsmouth Point, adjacent to the gate that separated the lawless crescent of land from the rest of the town. It was slanted and timber-framed, squeezed in on both sides by hovels and bawdy houses, the epicentre of a rampart of debauchery and vice that glowered over the Solent's crashing grey waves. It hummed with the sounds of humanity; and Marek Nowak embraced it like a lover.

It had all started with a game of Ruff wherein the Turk, boatswain of a Portuguese slaver up from Senegambia, had won a deal of money at Marek's expense. That, of course, had all been by the Polish gunner's design, culminating in an escalation of stakes and coin that had climaxed with a final, lucrative challenge. Fists in place of cards. *Give me the chance to win it back, my friend. Double or nothing!*

Now, the better part of twenty minutes later, as the grimacing Turk spat a crimson gobbet onto the clotted shavings, Marek decided that enough was enough. It was time to collect his winnings. He squinted through the pungent pall of sot weed smoke. The sky outside had been pale grey when he had stepped over the Jolly Sailor's foot-worn threshold but now he could see only the room's glowing reflection in the black windows. Somewhere in the background the fiddle played on. The attack was low when it came. A lunge for Marek's midriff, the intention to hoist him bodily into the air and slam him to earth but Marek sidestepped, giving his opponent a shove so that he staggered past. The pair spun together, joined once again. Marek evaded a hammering right, the air pulsing at his ear and planted one of his own on the end of the boatswain's chin, snapping back the sinewy neck. The Turk, the taller of the two, rocked rearward to keep his feet and shook his head like a rain-drenched dog, dark droplets scattering from the matted ends of his long hair. The crowd yowled their appreciation. He put a knuckle to his chin as if checking it had not shattered, grinned crookedly from behind black stubble and spat a globule of tainted spittle onto the sawdust between them.

Marek snuck a downward glance, catching the bright wink of a couple of teeth and slid his tongue around his mouth to confirm they were not his own. Satisfied, he twisted his torso to present the smallest target for the Turk's superior reach, thrust his left foot out in front and bounced gently on his toes, ignoring the exhausted pleas of his aching thighs. His heart raced, his limbs felt white-hot, his swollen fists numb.

The Turk came again, his muscular frame gliding like a ghoul in the hellish torchlight, the crowd roaring him on. Marek dodged a left jab but could not avoid the heavy straight right that followed. He juddered back, stamping his feet to make sure he still controlled them. He could feel a patch at the corner of his mouth already beginning to swell, spat thickly as the Turk had spat and then they came together again. The Turk swayed around Marek's punch, came inside the range of his fists and grasped Marek's head, grappling at his ears, holding, twisting, forcing him down as if trying to drown him in an invisible pool. Marek could smell the Turk, taste the bloody sweat that showered them both and the pain at the base of his neck told him he would soon crumple. He lashed twice at the taller man's wire-haired midriff to little effect and launched upwards, clubbing the back of his skull into the Turk's face. Bone crunched, skin split, new blood fountained. Only when Marek pushed away did he see that the blood was the Turk's, the man's nose and mouth smashed to a gnarled mess, his bulbous fists clawing ineffectually as he reeled away.

The mob shrieked. Marek gave chase, hands locking at the Turk's arm and waist as his opponent floundered unsighted, mewing like a wounded calf. Marek dipped, twisted at the hips, wrenching hard and the Turk lurched off his feet, barrelling over Marek's dropped shoulder. Marek went with him, letting the bigger man's momentum take him and he left the ground too, tumbling onto the hapless boatswain so that he landed with an elbow driven hard into the dazed fighter's windpipe. The mob bellowed their delight and chagrin and from the corner of his eye Marek could see the glint of metal as coins slipped between avaricious palms. He rolled away, gasping. The Turk was clutching his neck, a drainpipe gargle easing between split lips.

Marek hauled himself to his feet. A grossly corpulent man – the local butcher if Marek recalled correctly – waddled into the makeshift ring and began the count. His was the role of fight custodian, employed to keep decorum when all around lusted for blood and violence. Steadily and with the echo of every witness's voice, the numbers climbed.

The Turk did not.

Then came a torrent of noise as the half-minute mark was reached. The Turk's second crouched over the prone form, pleading with him to stand but to no avail.

Hands came then, grasping Marek's drenched arms and holding them aloft. The pain descended, as it always did, fast at the heels of a fight finished. Marek was vaguely aware of his opponent beginning to stir, rocking to the side to vomit. He felt himself sway a little and a trio of barely pubescent pot-boys gathered around to bolster his bulk like snot-nosed buttresses. He waved them away in irritation, totting up his teeth again, just to be sure and made his way over to one of the tables his men had commandeered. They cheered him as ever and Louis, his oldest comrade, pushed a slopping pot of ale into his distended hand.

After slaking his thirst, his gaze fell upon the one member of the group manifestly not enjoying himself. "What did you think?"

The stocky but sallow adolescent stared, eyes wide as plates, around the smoky room. "You won."

"Good money to be made at the prize play, boy." Marek grinned as he followed the dour youth's gaze. "An education, yes?"

"It is a vile place," Botolph Spendlove said with revulsion. He rubbed a hand over eyes as bruised as Marek's, as if he might wipe away the sinful scenes. "A lewd place."

"That it is, boy," Marek said. "One of my favourite places on God's earth."

"Why are we here?"

"Spice Island lies outside the town boundary. Law extends only as far as the wall and gate, yonder. To lodge in the town invites the tentacles of your Puritan Parliament to entwine us, constrict us. But here? Here we are kings."

"Spice Island? They store spice here?"

Marek guffawed. "It is so named for its..." he pursed his lips as he sought the apt word, "*flavoursome* ways."

Botolph screwed up his mouth as if he tasted something putrid. "Drink, cards and pugilism."

"More than that, boy," Marek answered with relish. "So much more."

Botolph looked up at the balcony, where a party of wide-skirted women loitered. One appeared to catch his eye, waving. He cast his gaze hurriedly to the table's ale-rings.

"Ha!" Marek exclaimed, raising his jar to the ladies, who chirped vulgar remarks in response, making him think of budgies at the bars of a cage. "You're going to die soon, boy. I do not wish it but I have made a pledge. Get up there and become a man before it is too late."

Botolph's frame stiffened, the vein at his neck pulsing visibly. "You'll not get away with this."

"Is that so?" Marek answered contemptuously. "Have you any inkling as to my value aboard ship? Laws of the land do not apply. All the while I can bring my gun to bear with accuracy and speed, I am General Blake's man and none may touch me." He leaned in, jabbing a finger into the youth's chest. "I want my property returned. *You* stole it, your *master* has it. If he elects to deprive me of what is mine, I will kill you dead. Make no mistake."

Botolph's eyes glistened with a wellspring of tears. "I have no knowledge of this property, sir. None at all. I'm a God fearing man, not a thief."

Marek almost hit the boy for that but he wished no more burning pain for knuckles that had already served him so well. He glanced at Botolph's crippled hand, resting at the table's edge. "Your affliction is my proof. Christ but I should let Duncan take his whip to you again." He was gratified to see the boy wince at the prospect, for his back was well-striped already. "You are in the employ of this renegade; this Ironside Highwayman."

"I'd never clapped eyes on him till moments before you stepped into the Lion," Botolph bleated.

Marek drank deeply, quaffing the ale and belching. He inspected his fists, opening and closing the damaged fingers tentatively. "It is the same tired protest you have bored me with a hundred times, boy. I am no longer listening. The highwayman will bring my property, or I will bring him a corpse. There can be no other way."

THURSDAY

Warblington Castle, Hampshire

It was still dark when Hobb took Whistler from his cell. He was cajoled across the potholed yard, as he had been the previous day but this time there was no rendezvous with great men in the slighted castle's lonesome tower. This time he was shown through one of the breaches in the crumbled walls, with only a single lamp, a scattering of stars and a sliver of moon to illuminate the way and everything obscured by the billowing fog of his own breath. His feet crunched on frost-hardened ground and his chest rasped with trepidation.

"You're for Petersfield," Hobb, as pungent as ever, explained as they walked. "God have mercy on you."

Before Whistler could reply, they were out in the clearing beyond the wall. Here, where the foot of the fortress's old boundary was banked by a deep drift of rubble, the land had been transformed into a place of construction; or, rather, demolition. Planks criss-crossed like miniature roads, so that barrow wheels might traverse the worst of the mud, while workbenches could be seen in the gloom alongside earth-filled gabions and half-a-dozen wagons. They were removing the stone and flint from the ancient fortification, he realised. Bringing down the curtain walls, breaking up the largest sections and carting it away for works elsewhere. The nearby village, presumably, though that was anyone's guess.

Horses whickered out in the darkness. Whistler squinted after the sounds. Hobb gestured with a chubby hand towards the treeline, some thirty paces distant. Before the trees there was a black shape, blotting out the trunks, its outline – a regular square with a domed roof – similar to a house but smaller than he would expect. As they drew closer, the sounds of the horses grew louder and the detail of the place gradually began to resolve. It was a dilapidated old pug mill house, once used in constructing the castle and now, he thought wryly, most likely a shelter for the men who tore the place down. It was also a shelter for the soldiers who would escort him to his death, for he could see the four big destriers now, tethered to stakes at the side of the pug mill. There was a thick coil of rope attached to one of their saddles and Whistler's guts lurched as he understood that that was surely intended for him.

"Over there, fellow," the voice of a man came suddenly from the murk, putting Whistler's heart in his mouth. He looked round, searching for the speaker. The man growled, "I said over there."

Whistler saw his outline, tall and lean but, before he could respond, he noticed it was Hobb that was hurrying to remove himself. All at once, he noticed the speaker's outstretched arm and the unmistakable shape of the pistol at its extent and he saw, too, that the weapon was indeed trained upon his erstwhile gaoler.

As Hobb moved, the glow of his lantern briefly snaked across the scene. Before it was extinguished, Whistler saw a face he had seen before. Green eyes, glinting like a prowling tomcat's behind that poised pistol. He glimpsed the interior of the pugmill beyond. The men crouching, huddled together in fear, wrists bound between knees.

He gaped at the man he had encountered outside the rain-lashed chapel at Idsworth. "You."

"Where is the bible? Come, Master Whistler, do not play the fool with me."

"A soldier has it," Whistler replied. "A black-haired bastard with a yellow scarf."

"Maddocks?"

Whistler shrugged. "Might have been."

The man with the pistol advanced a pace. "I have no particular desire to turn you loose. If you would have your freedom, you must earn it."

Whistler felt the bravado leak away. He nodded quickly. "Maddocks, aye. A colonel. He has it. The soldiers took it from my snapsack and that bastard had it when he questioned me. That's the last I saw of it, I swear."

"Used it to wipe their arses by now," another voice, crackling with age and coloured by the vowels of the westernmost counties, came from within the pugmill house. "Like as bliddy not."

Whistler laughed scornfully at that, despite his fear. "You think he's tossed a solid gold book into his fire?"

There was a pause, pregnant with realisation. "Gold?" Yet another new speaker from inside the shelter. This time a girl. Whistler wondered how many had come to affect this strangest of rescues. If a rescue was even what it was.

"You did not know?" he asked. "It is a bible. A popish one. All in Latin. Means nothing to me. But the bindings are covered in gold. Tis a very fine thing."

"Little wonder you pinched it," the old man's disembodied voice echoed in the dark.

"Aye, well, Jesu knows I wish I hadn't now."

The man with the green eyes said, "Is he there? Maddocks, is he still in the castle?"

*

"Jeremy?" Colonel Francis Maddocks called in response to the knock at his door. He was still in bed, the watery rays of a new dawn casting his chamber in dim grey.

"Sally, sir," came the reply from outside.

Startled to hear a female voice, Maddocks heaved his body up, tiredness counterbalanced by the relief of removing himself from the rudimentary straw palliasse that had made him itch most of the night. For the sake of decorum, he went to the wardrobe in which Jeremy, his usual servant, had hung his breeches and coat and quickly dressed before giving the order to enter. When the girl, who was about twelve at a guess, pushed open the door, he curtly demanded an explanation.

"An ague, sir," she explained, "God help him." She stepped into the room, bearing a large bowl of what he hoped would be warm water, a length of clean-looking linen draped over her forearm. "Taken to his bed. I have been sent in his stead."

Maddocks clapped his hands. "Smartly, then, for I cannot tarry."

She scurried to the low table beneath the room's only window and set down the bowl, folding the cloth into a neat square and placing it beside the water. "There's to be a hanging, so they say."

The casual tone annoyed Maddocks and he almost said as much but even the girl's impertinence could not dampen his mood. He gave an affirmative grunt as he bent over the bowl. "A prolific thief, aye." He splashed his face, pleased to discover that the water had, mercifully, been heated. When he straightened, using the cloth to dab away the trembling droplets from his nose and chin, he noticed Sally gazing absently out of the window that looked onto the castle's debris-strewn ward. "Not here, girl. It'll be done at Petersfield."

"Why, sir?"

"Propriety. Justice must be *seen* to be done in the appropriate manner. Even I cannot string an offender up from the nearest tree." Which was not strictly true, he thought, for he doubted any magistrate from here to Newbury would question the actions of Goffe's right-hand man but that did not mean Maddocks was keen to test the theory. "He'll meet his end at the town gallows on market day."

"Poor fellow," Sally said.

"We all must make our decisions in life and we all must carry the consequences." Maddocks cleaned his teeth with the linen, each tooth squeaking like an unoiled hinge as he buffed vigorously. When he was done, he dropped the cloth into the water and strode towards the door, fetching up his belt and weapons as he went. "Deal with that, girl," he commanded with a cursory wave back at the bowl. He took a sumptuous cape, the same colour as his capacious scarf, from a hook in the dark wainscoting. "I ride for Petersfield."

"To see justice done, sir?"

He could not help but smile at that. "Just so, Sally. Just so."

*

Near Widley, Hampshire

Star's lungs roared as he ran west.

Lyle leaned in, calling encouragement, urging the grey stallion to dredge more speed from legs that must have been growing heavier by the moment. But he could not relent. It was almost seven miles to Portsea Island and he had chosen to take the high road, over the hills, where the going was more hazardous but the lanes less conspicuous, which meant that a full gallop was impossible. And all the while the sun climbed out of the horizon at their backs.

Amelia clung on tight, squeezing Lyle's midriff, her cheek pressed against his back. He looked to his right, checking that Grumm and Tyrannous were managing to keep pace. Behind the Cornishman was Whistler. The deserter-turned-thief looked frailer than ever, as if the wispiest of breezes might topple him from the saddle. He seemed so feeble, so inconsequential, clinging to the former smuggler like a limpet on a rock and yet what chaos the man had wrought. What forces he had unwittingly unleashed. And now there was Maddocks. Lyle saw the colonel's face as he thundered along the track that was taking them up the chalky escarpment fringing the expansive harbours of Langstone and Portsmouth. His old comrade when they had fought under Ireton – ironsides together, zealous and triumphant – only to become his nemesis in the aftermath of Lyle's desertion and Alice's cruel death. Maddocks had hunted Lyle ever since, had chased him through forests and faced him at sword point and here he was again, dragged into Whistler's mess just as Lyle had been. Maddocks. The thought of him made Lyle shudder in the gloom. He was a reminder. Of a lost past and a futile future. And now Lyle would be forced to confront him again. Because soon, inevitably, the hunt would resume and Lyle would have to fight for his life.

*

Warblington Castle, Hampshire

"An ambush?"

The young cornet of horse, whose usual role of carrying his troop's colour had been superseded this dawn by an impromptu prisoner escort, blanched under the severe gaze of his colonel. "It was dark, sir," he bleated, putting Maddocks in mind of a frightened lamb. He pointed at the domed pugmill some twenty yards to his rear. "They came out of the mill shelter. Tied us up."

"And took the prisoner," Maddocks completed the sentence. He had already clambered into the saddle and fastened his freshly polished helm before hearing the chorus of alarmed voices coming from beyond the castle ward. Making for the sound at a swift canter, he had come upon a scene of confusion involving a routine foot patrol and the disarmed, bound and gagged wretches they had stumbled upon. Those humiliated creatures had turned out to be members of Maddocks's own unit, which was something of an embarrassment but when he had finally grasped the implication, he had a mind to run each and every one of them through. He twisted, finding his immediate subordinate in the gathering daylight. "Captain Beck? Who, in Christ's holy name, would do such a thing? Why?"

Beck, who had scurried out of his own lodgings behind a suspiciously half-clad stable boy, had only just managed to gather himself for the breathless inquest. Red at the jowls and sweating profusely, he panted, "Fellow thieves, sir?"

Maddocks awarded the suggestion the scorn-dripping sneer it deserved. "We have not encountered a modern-day Robin Hood, Captain." He went back to the shame-faced cornet. "What did the culprits look like?"

The cornet was busily rubbing his recently untied wrists. "They wore hoods, sir. It was dark."

"Try."

The cornet risked a look up. "Three of them."

Another of the prisoner detail, a youngster with a dark complexion and a pronounced squint, cleared his throat nervously. "Four."

The cornet nodded vigorously. "Aye, four, that's right. The leader was a man. About my height."

"Accent?" Maddocks asked.

The cornet shrugged. "Local, sir but-"

"But?" prompted Maddocks.

"His accomplices were unusual," the cornet ventured.

Maddocks shifted his weight impatiently. "How so? Come, boy, do not be timid."

"One was elderly," the cornet said. "That is to say, he had an old man's voice. And, I may be mistaken but I reckoned on two women."

That caught Maddocks's attention. He edged forwards, ignoring the cornet's flinch. "Women?"

The trooper with the squint said, "He ain't mistook, sir. Women, for certain. One was very young, at a guess."

And in that moment Maddocks knew. His heart seemed to plummet from his chest into his stomach and back again. "It is Lyle."

Beck, apparently composed now, said, "The Ironside Highwayman? But why would he bother with that raggedy pilferer?"

But Maddocks was not listening, because something else – something worse – had occurred to him. Not occurred. The realisation had stabbed him full in the guts. "My lodgings," he said absently, almost to himself as the connotations squawked and swirled like birds through his mind. Then, louder, "To my lodgings, Captain Beck, immediately!"

*

Portsmouth Point, Hampshire

Botolph Spendlove had always wanted to visit the coast. A product of the rolling hills, he had walked those high crests and squinted into a horizon dazzled by the sea more times than he could count but there had never been reason or occasion to brave the roads that would take a traveller to the nation's southern edge. The miles between Chalton and the Solent were lush and bucolic but they also negotiated challenging terrain and footpad-infested forests. His life, therefore, had been one of gentle downland and sleepy village, cosseted by parents who knew too much of the world to risk exposing their precious offspring to it and Botolph had been left to stew in his frustration and long for the chance to see soldiers and bustling streets and mighty warships.

Now Botolph had it all and wanted none. He was in the thick of it, the lively, dangerous and depraved horn of dry land that served England but was not truly part of her. Portsmouth Point. Spice Island. There were sailors and dockworkers here. Privateers and pirates, hawkers and pickpockets, smugglers and swindlers, fishermen and ferrymen, gamblers, drinkers, whores and their pimps. Out in the harbour there were the warships he had craved to see, billowing shrouds rigged to masts as tall as great oaks. The streets were a cacophony of shouts and laughter, of foreign tongues and strange faces from all corners of God's creation, while the pungent scents of a hundred exotic spices mingled to make even the sharpest breeze heady and intoxicating. It was everything he could ever have imagined. And all he wanted was to go home.

"Come, lad," Duncan said, cuffing Botolph hard enough to make him stumble.

Botolph barely managed to keep his feet. He could hear the mocking laughter of his captors at his back. He could feel the heat of humiliation rise through his face and his swollen eye sockets began to pulse. As he straightened, he risked a sideways glance at the huge Scotsman, noticing with a shudder how Duncan pointedly fingered the knotted coil of leather at his belt. The wounds that striped his spine began to burn at the sight of it, reminding him of the first hours after his capture, when these evil men had attempted to extract information that simply was not his to impart. He noted, too, that with his free hand Duncan picked at the scab on his chin. It gave him a glimmer of pleasure to know that it was Amelia who had inflicted the wound.

Perhaps catching a shadow of defiance in the hostage's look, Duncan advanced with his black gums bared, unhooking the whip in one deft motion. He unfurled it, working his wrist so that it rippled from handle to tip. Botolph shied away, shielding himself with his arms, though bitter experience told him it would prove futile.

"Duncan!" Marek's harsh voice brought the Scot up short. "I want him in one piece."

The Scot furnished Botolph with a sour look but he stayed his hand nonetheless, letting the others amble past as he coiled the leather once more. They were on the move, the gunners, bleary eyed and ill-tempered after a night of debauchery. They had vacated the Jolly Sailor at dawn and now made their way north, intending to take new lodgings at an inn situated flush against the dock, there to await the ship's boat that would soon berth for the agreed rendezvous. *Diamond* was to sail back to Cadiz in a matter of weeks, Botolph had learned and all hands were expected back on deck to begin preparations.

Marek came alongside him, nodding at the cobbles to invite him to walk. "He does not like you. The book is," he waved a meaty hand, knuckles distended like knots on a branch, "priceless to us. But I must keep you whole so that that *skurwysyn* keeps his side of the bargain."

"Why do you call him that name?"

"*Skurwysyn*? Bastard. Whoreson. Your master-"

"He is not my master, you must believe me, I-"

"Your master," Marek said firmly, "is the worst kind of devil. A thief, for certain but also a liar."

Botolph abandoned the plea that had been forming on his tongue, for he could see plainly enough that Marek would brook no argument. Instead he gazed about the busy thoroughfare. "I have never been here before."

"Spice Island?"

"Portsmouth." He thought back to their brief conversation the night before. "You said it was an education."

"I was right?"

"You were." He looked up at the big gun captain, a heavy stone forming in his stomach. "How will I die?"

"The water," Marek replied, the frankness of his tone making Botolph shudder. "It is painless, so they tell me. I could make it worse for you, boy." His voice darkened in warning. "Do not give me reason."

"I will not," Botolph said hurriedly.

"Will he come?"

"This highwayman?" Botolph shrugged helplessly. "How should I know?"

Marek laughed at that. "You have spirit, boy, I concede. You'd make a fine hand aboard *Diamond*." He shook his head when Botolph made to speak. "Alas, that can never be. Your master has my book. I must be seen to fulfil my promise."

"But if he does not come with this book," Botolph said, "he will not be here to witness my death. What can be gained?"

"Plenty will bear witness, boy. Word will reach him and he will know."

*

Portsdown Hill

"I wondered why those bastards kept to their fire," Whistler said as the horses drew up on the escarpment's crest. The sun was fully visible now, the day cold but bright. "In the yard at Petersfield. Why not lodge under a roof, I thought? If not the farmhouse, then surely one of the stables."

"Sailors are not readily welcome," Lyle said as he gazed down on the flat expanse of Portsea Island. The view snatched the air from his lungs. The coastal plain stretched off to sea, a patchwork of field and marsh, road and hedgerow, with the rooftops of Portsmouth dark in the distance, a charcoal outline against the horizon.

Behind him, Amelia spoke. “For their rough manners?”

Whistler laughed. “For their poxed pizzles, Mistress!”

“That’s enough,” Lyle ordered. He was still staring into the distance, where land met water, examining the forest of bare masts that sprouted like black shoots from the glittering Solent, marking the bustling harbour and dockyard and, further out, the anchorage at Spithead, black hulls of the biggest vessels smudging the sky. Blake’s great warships were there, sheltered from all but south-easterly winds as they awaited the order to set shrouds and sail for Spain. *Diamond* would be among them. He tried to guess which.

“And a man has more than thirst to be slaked,” Whistler was saying with obvious relish, “after many a month at sea. Any home with daughters to protect does not open the door to such travellers, no matter how weary they may be.”

Lyle tore himself away from the ships and turned Star so that the grey stallion faced Grumm’s black gelding. “Down you get.”

When Grumm did not move, the light of understanding showed in Whistler’s small eyes. His mouth dropped. “You mean to strand me?” His head jerked left and right, like a rat surveying potential routes of escape. “On this bloody hill in the middle o’ nowhere?”

“Hardly nowhere,” Lyle said. He pointed north, to the breeze-rippled pastures beyond Whistler and Grumm. “You’ll find the Southwick road yonder.”

“I will apologise to the lady, sir, I-”

Lyle cut him off with a shake of his head. “I owe you nothing but a thrashing, sirrah, so I would consider yourself fortunate that I am willing to turn you loose."

"I shall starve," Whistler opined, his tone growing shriller with desperation.

"Here." Lyle produced a small pouch from his saddle and tossed it to Whistler, who caught it with his scarred hand. "Get some food in your belly when the moment is opportune. But get away from here without delay. There'll be soldiers on this road soon enough."

The thief weighed the money in his ruined palm and slid out of the saddle, leaving Grumm to make theatre of stretching his shoulders, as if the weight of the world had been lifted from them. Whistler asked, "Where shall I go?"

"I care only that I do not look upon your face again," Lyle said.

Whistler glanced at the purse. "I can arrange that."

Lyle nodded. "See that you do."

They took the bridleway that led them south towards the vast island. Steep and winding, it cut a swathe through the white and green face of Portsdown Hill, small chunks of chalk skittering before them, kicked up by the horses' hooves. The slope was carpeted in long grass and thick brier patches, broken up by stands of trees and through the branches they could make out the rooftops of the villages nestling like mushrooms at the hill's foot.

"Wymering," Lyle said, indicating the buildings. "With Cosham beyond."

He felt Amelia lift her head from his shoulder to take an interest. "That is where we leave the horses?"

"And meet Bella, God willing."

They rode on. Resisting the use of their spurs to save the horses but always urging the tired beasts to push, for the road at their backs would not remain empty forever. Folk were abroad, though it was still early. Small children played and shrieked in the trees and Lyle's party were forced to negotiate their way through increasing amounts of traffic. Heavily loaded wagons, making hard work of the cloying terrain, travelled in the opposite direction, interspersed by a small flock of sheep, a sack-laden donkey and a gaggle of stick-driven geese, all noisily vying for space as their owners looked to do business on the first dry day for some time.

When they reached the village, Lyle made directly for the imposing whitewashed façade of Wymering Manor, a place so ancient that folk often found the detritus of Roman habitation in its gardens and cellars. From that landmark he was able to resurrect the lie of the land from memory and quickly located an inn just around the corner. The Bull & Gate was a modest, single storey affair but he recalled that it had adequate stabling and a discreet owner. He was forced to pay over the odds to the ostlers and landlord for a guarantee of security and anonymity, "But the crossing will be guarded by soldiers," he explained to a disgruntled Grumm, "so we must travel inconspicuously."

Bella arrived soon afterwards, having taken the low coast road around Langstone Harbour. "Ain't seen the buggers," she replied, swinging out of the saddle, as Lyle took hold of Newt's head collar and enquired as to any sign of trouble. "But I'd wager they've noticed the book's vanished by now."

A high-sided dray, drawn by two meaty cart-horses and driven by a portly bald man, with a slab face and thick neck rolls, came to a halt about forty paces away. The vehicle was packed full of tightly bound hemp bales and Lyle watched as the driver leaned back on his bench and lit a pipe. "You found it, then?" he asked Bella with a wry smile.

"Simple enough. Kept it in a little travelling chest." Bella gave an impish cackle. "Men like that do not need to hide their things. They're untouchable, ain't they? Who'd dare burgle them?" She winked at Amelia, who was watching with apparent astonishment as the little girl produced a gold-bound bible from her saddlebag. "Don't occur there might be a cuckoo in the nest."

Lyle took the gleaming object and thrust it into the folds of his cloak. "How fares the lad?"

Bella pulled an exaggeratedly sad expression. "Poor Jeremy!" She tapped her knuckles at her temple. "A sore head, I shouldn't wonder but he'll live. Now then," she clapped her hands and looked expectantly at Lyle, "we cannot stroll onto Portsea Island, Samson, so I hope to God you've cooked up a decent plan."

*

Portsbridge Fort, above Ports Creek, Hampshire

Maddocks dug his spurs into his mount's heaving flanks as the fort came into view. He had led a hastily mustered troop of forty out of Warblington Castle in something akin to blind panic, sending half up and over the hills, the rest staying with him on the marshy coast road and now they came together again in a flurry of hoof-beats and bellows. No one, it seemed, had been captured, nor so much as spotted. With frustration turning to rage, he directed his vengeful harquebusiers towards the narrow crossing onto Portsea Island.

Maddocks had known they would not find the book as soon as he had learned of Lyle's involvement. Why would such a man embroil himself with the likes of Whistler, the ever-sceptical Captain Beck had asked? The answer had rung like a bell in Maddocks's head. The Vulgate bible. And even as he had wrenched his horse's head about and galloped back into the decrepit castle's inner ward, he had known the golden book would not be where he had left it. There was nothing for it, except to rouse the men and hunt the malefactors to ground.

The high earthwork loomed above the road, dominating the landscape as it had for at least two centuries. The passage of time had weathered the rampart, stealing a few feet from the summit and filling parts of the defensive ditch but all that was counterweighted easily enough by the rows of fresh stakes, pale at the newly sharpened tips, that protruded like the teeth of some monstrous maw. The fort was shaped like a star, its high bulwarks reminiscent of the sconces Maddocks had seen at London, Worcester and Newark, yet this formidable obstacle was not designed to conduct or obstruct a siege but rather to protect the single crossing onto Portsea Island, thus giving landward protection to the crucial naval installations beyond.

Maddocks hauled on the reins as he reached the broad timber bridge over the ditch, noting the ominous black muzzles of half-a-dozen heavy guns on the rampart immediately above. His horse whinnied as it wheeled, great clods of mud flinging in all directions and he barked at the pair of sentries standing before the huge open gates. Their eyes wandered over him, taking in the cut of his expensive clothes, the gleam of his polished plate and the lion's head embroidered onto the saffron scarf. His pennant was coming, lofted on a long pole by a young cornet but they did not need to see the device to know with whom they were dealing. They stepped aside smartly and the troopers thundered across the ditch and into the open expanse of the fort, which proved to be a flat plateau containing a gravel track and a single wooden building that served as the soldiers' quarters. Told to take their ease, the troopers found space to dismount and went to sit on the grass, fishing hard biscuit, dried meat or wads of fragrant sotweed from their bags.

On the far side of the fort, in a reflection of the landward gates, the doorway above the creek gaped open, the flanking guards taking a markedly languid approach to their duties. Maddocks, still mounted, approached them, Captain Beck a few yards in his wake. "Riders," he called down to a swarthy sergeant who leaned nonchalantly against a halberd that was decorated with brightly coloured tassels. "Three, perhaps four. Have you seen them?"

The sergeant sucked at his black whiskers for a moment, then gave a noncommittal twitch of the shoulders. "Seen plenty o' folk since sun-up, sir."

"This party," Maddocks replied brusquely, "is led by a criminal. Tall, green eyes, into his late twenties. He is accompanied by a haggardly old clapperdudgeon and two females."

The sergeant glanced in amusement at his trio of subordinates. "Circus troupe, by the sounds of it," he ventured in an accent native to the West Midlands, "though we haven't seen the like."

Maddocks sucked his teeth in frustration. "Brigands, all"

"Lady outlaws, sir?" The sergeant's surprise was evident and he looked round at his men. "We'd not let in that kind of miscreant, would we, boys? Goodness me, no."

Captain Beck asked, "What think you, Colonel? Back on the road?"

Maddocks adjusted his cloak, buying time for consideration. He let his horse walk between the sentries and under the arch, to look upon the mossy blocks of stone that formed the bridge onto the island. Either side, the waters of the creek ran fast and murky, foaming thick where it parted around the base of each pier. He twisted to look back at Beck, who had come up to occupy the arch. "If Lyle had merely freed that flea-bitten little weasel then maybe. But he stole the bible."

Beck's fleshy face screwed into an expression of incredulity. "He's gone elsewhere, sir. Up country to sell his ill-gotten loot."

"Marek Nowak has one of the highwayman's gang," Maddocks answered, his tone firming with rapidly increasing certainty. "Lyle will not stand for such a thing, I'd stake my life on it. He has stolen the bible in order to return it. Exchange it for his fellow criminal."

"Then where is the blackguard?" Beck said in exasperation.

They were interrupted by the sergeant's voice, orders spilling loud and fast as he hurried to direct newly arrived traffic towards the crossing. Maddocks went back to look upon the commotion. Several wagons, stacked high with wool bales, had come down off the hill, it seemed and, funnelling through the earthwork, they would now need the cavalrymen to move aside. Between them and with the sergeant's profuse apologies as accompaniment, Maddocks and Beck managed to corral their resting troopers onto their horses and into a double file. When they were ready to ride, the colonel let his cornet come up, raising the colour for all to see and led them in a clattering chorus across the creek and onto Portsea Island. The hunt would resume in earnest.

Because the wagons had given him an idea.

*

Portsmouth, Hampshire

It had been years since Lyle had ventured down to the coast, where the Solent lashed the shore and the gulls wheeled and cackled but Portsmouth was just as he remembered. As the afternoon leaked away, the light gradually washing out, the cart had squeezed its way into the town, waved through the ornate gateway that was set into a huge, flag-topped and crenelated bastion, the jaded-looking sentries offering the most cursory of glances as they processed a line of vehicles that ran into the dozens. The muddy road beyond the long defensive wall had instantly become paved, sporadic steadings giving way to tightly packed terraces, thatch-work replaced by tiles in an evident effort to negate the effects of fire. The streets were busy, the bellows of barrow boys and basket wielders vying with purveyors of ribbon and string, eggs and milk, apples and leather and shoes.

All this Lyle and his companions heard, rather than witnessed, for theirs was a journey glimpsed via the chinks of light between their covering of hemp bales. In other circumstances the commandeering of the vehicle would have been a source of deep regret, for he had genuinely sympathised with the unwitting driver. The poor fellow had been taking his ease, eyes firmly shut, as he drank the tobacco smoke and let his cares drift into the crisp air. What a rude awakening it had been to feel the cruel press of cold metal as Lyle had pushed his pistol's twin muzzles into the bulging folds of skin at the nape of the terrified man's neck.

"You're travelling to the docks," Lyle had whispered into the man's rapidly reddening ear. It had not been a question, for where else was a huge consignment of hemp destined?

"Aye," had been the murmured response, from one too frightened to nod, "to the new ropery."

And so, with the promise that the driver's brains would be splattered over his cargo if he gave them away, the Ironside Highwayman and his accomplices became stowaways.

"Baltic hemp, out of Königsberg," the driver, doing his utmost to convey a calmness that he cannot possibly have felt, had explained as the chief sentry at the Portsbridge Fort had questioned him. "Comes into Port of London and I takes it out to Chatham, then down here. Makes the finest cordage on God's earth."

"I'm sure it does," had been the bored-sounding reply and

then, to Lyle's palpable relief, they were out and away, the dray's wheels bouncing alarmingly over the stone bridge and onto the low-lying island, immediately picking up the road that would snake its way through village and field, all the way to Portsmouth and the sea. The gaps between the bales allowed Lyle to see the high bulwarks of the fort sink into the distance, eventually replaced by the scarp of Portsdown Hill and an empty sky that was a uniform grey. Then it had been a matter of nervous patience. Of waiting and listening. But, despite the occasional pocket of heavy traffic and a couple of mud-stuck wheels, they had made it to the town without significant hindrance.

Portsmouth itself was a bastion of civilisation at the southwest corner of Portsea Island. As the dray bounced and juddered along High Street, the frontages of shops and taverns raced past Lyle's little peephole in a blur. Fishmongers were abundant, along with net makers and boatwrights. There were at least two coopers, a large smithy, a chandlery, a bakery and so many more. Storehouses for raw fleeces stood shoulder to shoulder with brewhouses and tanneries and everywhere folk walked and rode, clogging the street, while sailors stood in the doorways of drinking dens and young lads darted hither and thither bearing parcels, goods and messages. The stink of the place reminded Lyle of London, a pungent concoction of seaweed and sewage, while the noise of lowing livestock and haggling shop-keeps overlaid all.

They trundled on, Lyle silently noting The Greyhound tavern, in which the Duke of Buckingham had been murdered during the old king's reign. It was the first of his signposts. In quick succession came the second, the large edifice of the Guildhall, its painted timbers dark in the fading light. Immediately he thumped a fist against the side of the cart.

"Here," he whispered to the others, "is where Master

Spendlove should be."

Without further discussion, they waited for the dray to rumble off the cobbles and into a muddy side road, where it immediately came to a halt. Cautiously they pushed the bales aside and emerged like larvae from a dung hill, wriggling free and shuffling on their backsides to the end of the cart. The driver, eager to be rid of his unwanted cargo, had already leapt down from his seat and unhooked the rear panel, so that the four stowaways could jump clear. With Lyle's contrite thanks ringing in his ears, the man closed the vehicle, gave a surly nod and clambered up.

In moments the huge dray had juddered into life, hemp bales tumbling and resettling like a disturbed leaf pile as it rounded the corner. In the street, all fell to silence. Rows of narrow, two-storey homes flanked the strip of mud on which Lyle and his companions found themselves.

"What now, Samson?" Bella asked.

Lyle opened his mouth to answer but someone else spoke first.

"Praise be," Wardley Spendlove said as he came out of one of the low doorways. His mouth twitched into a smile at Lyle, growing to a delighted beam when his gaze fell on one of the other faces. "Oh, Jesu, it is my Amelia. Praise be."

A tear welled at the corner of Amelia's eye, trembling there for a moment, before plunging down her cheek. "Papa," she whispered and ran to embrace him.

*

Night had well and truly fallen when Maddocks called off the search.

The colonel, as a matter of efficacy as well as dignity, had perched atop his skittish, snorting destrier and overseen a methodical afternoon's work while his troopers, on foot and cursing their ill-fortune, had waylaid as many wagons, traps and coaches as they could manage along the road from Wymering to Portsmouth. Maddocks had ridden up and down the wide thoroughfare, scanning every face, for only he would know his former friend on sight. But the stretch, however flat and unobstructed, was all of five miles, busy as any road outside the capital and the task's futility had quickly become apparent.

The troop filed through the gate at Portsmouth's main bastion as a bright half-moon, smudged by fingers of cloud, spread silvery film over houses and battlements. With Maddocks, Captain Beck and the cornet at the fore, they made their beleaguered way south, along St Thomas Street to the huge Romanesque church dedicated to the martyred Archbishop of Canterbury after whom the street was named.

"Took some iron during the wars," Beck said.

Maddocks glanced at his captain, realising the man was staring at St Thomas's large central tower. It was difficult to see in the gathering gloom but the high walls were jagged in places, as if giant jaws had taken great bites out of the stonework. He nodded. "True enough. From our side, God forgive us, when the king's men held the town. The malignants used the tower as a lookout post, for its vantage cannot be bettered." When they reached the church, he signalled for the column to veer left, cutting across the junction with High Street so that they headed south and east. "There was no alternative but for our gunners over at Gosport to subject the place to bombardment. The nave was dire harmed too, though I pray one day the Parliament will see to its improvement."

"The conflict spared no place," Beck muttered sombrely.

"Nor any person," Maddocks replied, unable to keep his mind from wandering to a former major in Henry Ireton's regiment. That man had been his ally once, trusted and valued but the events of the last decade had tainted him, corrupted him. It was a point of bitter regret for Maddocks but also of stinging betrayal. Even as he considered the souring of his relationship with Samson Lyle, his heart hardened, his resolve to capture the fugitive setting a new fire in his belly. "See there?"

Beck touched at heel to his horse and the animal quickened to keep pace with the colonel. "Domus Dei?"

"As was," Maddocks confirmed. They were approaching another impressive complex of buildings, some constructed in the pale dressed stone of Norman churches and castles, while others, like new buds sprouting from an ancient bough, were made up of timber and brick, painted brilliant white and adorned with huge windows, ornate chimney stacks and smartly tiled roofs. It was an incongruous hotch-potch of a site, set just within the easternmost line of the town wall, all enclosed by a well-tended green and several large, timber outbuildings. "Domus Dei," he repeated the name. "God's House. An almshouse and hospice before the Dissolution."

"The new parts are the Governor's residence?"

"A modern mansion," Maddocks said with distaste. "Slapped on the side. Government House, we are now to call it." He shrugged. "Whatever its name, it has roaring hearths and plenty of good stabling. We shall dwell therein and see to our cursed quarry on the morrow."

Beck, evidently content with the prospect of food and lodgings, sat straighter in the saddle. "How will we locate him?"

"Marek Nowak. It is too late, too damned dark to ransack every smuggler's haunt and drinking ken in Portsmouth but he and his men will be here somewhere and they'll prove a sight simpler to track down than Lyle and his little parcel of thieves." They turned into the grounds of the Governor's House, hooves suddenly loud on the cinder path that would take them to the gates. "Tomorrow, Captain," Maddocks said, mood beginning to lighten with renewed hope. "We shall prevail, have no doubt. Find the sailor and we shall find the outlaw."

*

"They lodge at The Bridge tavern," Wardley Spendlove said as he took his place on a low bench, leaning over his knees to enjoy the warming flames. "I followed them all the way to its threshold." His nose and upper lip crumpled in disgust. "It is out on The Point, so called Spice Island by the locals. A den of iniquity, full of houses of ill-repute, overflowing with strong ale and more illegal stills than you could possibly sup from. It is a lewd, violent place of danger and temptation."

Eustace Grumm, at the other end of the bench, gave a salacious chuckle. "Sounds wondrous."

It was pitch dark outside, the clarity of the night sky letting a hard chill descend. The only light in the fisherman's home came from the hearth, dancing and crackling as logs blackened while hands and faces were held out for as long as could be tolerated. Bella and Amelia sat cross-legged on the rushes, either side of the chimney breast, while squeezed on the bench between the two old men, Lyle asked, "What is Botolph's condition?"

Spendlove's features tightened at whatever unhappy image the question conjured. "He lives," he said simply.

Lyle took his roasting palms away from the heat and rubbed them across his freshly shaved cheeks. "Then let us consider extricating the fellow."

"Thorny task, that," replied the owner of their new bolthole. In order to safeguard the man, who lived alone in what was a clean and well-appointed dwelling of just two rooms, Lyle had introduced him simply as Tom. Distant kin to Lyle's late wife, the fisherman – as white-bearded as Grumm, if not nearly as thin – had welcomed Spendlove when the old man had appeared at his door. Now that the group had come together under his roof, he provided a much-needed fire, fresh bread and a dish of turbot and mushrooms. They would sleep on the floor, for there were no beds to spare but that mattered not a jot now that they were warm and full-bellied.

Lyle glanced across at Tom, who sat in a cushioned chair nearest the hearth, a clay pipe dangling from the corner of his mouth. "How so?"

The fisherman sucked the pale stem, a stream of smoke tumbling from his nose and peered back with milky blue eyes that were sagging and wet, reminding Lyle of half-open clams. "The Bridge is out on The Point."

Lyle sketched a map in his mind's eye. At the westernmost edge of the town, beyond the main defences, he remembered there was a small tidal bay that was almost entirely enclosed by a crescent-shaped spit of land. That spur, Portsmouth Point, being a landing place for many of the sailors coming ashore from the Spithead anchorage, had its own gate in order to protect the town from interlopers. "Do they man the wall there?"

The fisherman dragged on his pipe again, speaking through the roiling smoke screen. "They do."

Grumm looked across at Spendlove. "You got in."

"One man, infirm and unarmed," Spendlove replied, "may slip through Point Gate unhindered but you?" he said pointedly, shaking his head, "With your guns and your blades?"

Grumm sat back, pulling a sour face. Lyle stared into the flames for inspiration. "Is there another way in?"

Tom leaned forwards, the bench lurching alarmingly and knocked his pipe bowl against the brick of the hearth. "Aye, I'd say there is."

FRIDAY

Oyster Street formed the western extremity of Portsmouth, hugging the foreshore, the town on one side, the grey waters of the harbour on the other. It was a commercial hub, smartly paved and packed with taverns and shops, with a huge pipe manufactory in the centre that seemed to hum with life, workers coming and going like bees at a gigantic hive.

Lyle took it all in as they walked south in the fledgling dawn, painfully aware that it would only take one person to recognise him and the day would quickly tumble to chaos. They moved in single file, Lyle, Amelia, Spendlove and Bella, leaving plenty of space in between so as not to be perceived as a group. Tom, leading the way, slowed his pace. "That there's the Camber," he called over his shoulder.

Lyle looked to his right, along the alleyway between two pubs. He could see water on the far side but it was evidently not the harbour proper, for a low-lying strip of land, complete with its own quay and buildings seemed to cut it off. This, then, was the bay he remembered, known locally as the Camber and soon he found himself hooking a right, down another of the alleys to leave Oyster Street at his back. They passed several warehouses, full, no doubt, of goods to be brought into the wharves further along the shoreline. Then they emerged at the water's edge. Here there was a timber jetty set upon slime-clothed stone footings that might have been centuries old. It jutted into the mouth of the Camber, the dock and quay of The Point lying across the water, immediately opposite the two structures separating the bay from the rest of Portsmouth Haven. On the far side, set a short way back from the quay, Lyle saw a large tavern, its name daubed in thick letters above the door. "The Bridge," he said aloud.

Beside him, the fisherman grunted. "Not a place I'd choose to visit." He paced along the length of the jetty, indicating a small boat that was tied alongside. "Here. Your vessel awaits."

*

"You mean to tell me that Samson Lyle has not made contact?"

Francis Maddocks stood over the Polish sailor, keeping his clenched fists collected at his back so as not to show his bubbling annoyance. It had taken less than an hour of daylight to locate the gun crew, for he had dispatched a score of troopers to the various inns and brothels dotting the community and such men were neither subtle, nor in hiding. Early hope, however, had quickly turned sour upon discovering that Lyle had not come to make the exchange. The revelation was as confusing as it was bitter.

Marek perched on the edge of a low palliasse to pull on his boots. Behind him the bed sheets were heaped in a haphazard hillock, out of which a slender leg protruded. "What concern is it of yours, Colonel?"

"Word reached me that you had kidnapped a citizen of the Commonwealth."

Marek shook his head, still fiddling with a boot. "Untrue."

"And that the taking of said citizen was enacted as a matter of ransom, in lieu of the return of a certain book. The Roman scriptures, no less."

Now Marek looked up, his expression impassive. If the colonel and his heavily armed riders, milling about the downstairs taproom, were intimidating, he did not show it. "I would not know."

"Scriptures," Maddocks went on, "stolen by one Samson

Lyle, former officer in the army of Parliament, latterly and commonly known as the Ironside Highwayman."

The woman in the bed rolled over, exposing a little more skin as she made a drowsy mewing sound. Marek ignored her, though he caught Maddocks' furtive glance and gave a wry smile. "She is available, Colonel. I'm done with her."

Maddocks felt himself colour and cleared his throat angrily. "I know Lyle will make contact with you, Master Nowak. I would simply see the criminal dead. I am not your enemy."

"I wish only to rest here," Marek said, pushing up from the bed to loom over the cavalryman, his myriad scars a map of violence across his ruddy face, "until my transport arrives at the dock."

"And when will that be?"

"This afternoon. A boat will be dispatched from the ship *Diamond*."

"I will not interfere with your plans." He glanced again at the mound in the bed, lowering his voice. "I care not for the man you have allegedly abducted. I want only to see Samson Lyle dance the Tyburn jig."

Marek ran a hand through his hair, the gold hoop glinting in his ear and went to a side table where he perused an impressive array of weapons. "I intend to board my ship, Colonel. Nothing more. Nothing less."

Maddocks ground his teeth so hard he feared they might shatter. He nodded sharply. "Thank you, Master Nowak," he said tersely, "and good sailing."

Maddocks glowered as he strode back to the waiting mounts. He could not have expected any help from Nowak but still the man's pigheaded silence was infuriating. It had occurred to him that full disclosure of the recent whereabouts of the Vulgate bible might coax some semblance of cooperation from the slab-faced Pole but, equally, a confession that he had possessed the book at Warblington might have had the opposite effect.

"Petersfield, sir?" Captain Beck asked as Maddocks gave a slight shake of the head.

The colonel adjusted his long cape and took his horse's reins from one of his troopers. He looked up at the plump form of Beck, high in the saddle. "It is not over until that pirate and his motley gaggle of rakehells are aboard their warship. We wait and we watch."

Beck stared out at the weed-flecked surface of the Camber. "To the Governor's House, then?"

"To Point Gate," Maddocks replied once he had hauled himself up, pushing his toes through the stirrups. "We'll search every soul attempting to pass through. If we can intercept the sly fox before he so much as reaches that foreign pope's-turd, then we get Lyle *and* the golden book. Marek Nowak can do what he likes with the Chalton boy, as long as I have the honour of handing General Goffe Lyle's head on a plate."

Beck grunted in black amusement. "A golden book and a silver platter, eh?"

"And a dead highwayman," Maddocks said. "Pray Jesu."

*

The carter muttered irritably to himself as the two watchmen emerged from guard huts set at either side of the wide entranceway. There were large wooden gates behind them, strengthened with thick, black iron strips but they had been jammed open for the day's expected traffic. The watchmen were Army personnel, pristine in the red coats and polished plate of the Lord Protector and both carried polearms topped with vicious-looking steel that immediately crossed to block the way. One of them, a burly man with a thick red beard, asked what business would concern the carter within the Commonwealth Dockyard.

"Shite," the carter answered.

The guards exchanged a glowering glance. The red-bearded man shouldered his polearm and took a step closer. "Mind your manners, my wizened friend, or pass you shall not."

The carter gave a high-pitched cackle that made both sentries start. "Shite, lad! Dung! I am here for your dung! That is to say, the dung of your chooks."

The second soldier – tall and gangly, with a prominent nose that glistened at the tip – tapped his helmet with a gloved knuckle. "Scrambled wits, Corporal."

"I'll scramble your wits, boy," the carter hissed, leaning forward above his mud-spattered palfrey, "and that dripping beak besides!"

The tall soldier advanced, his expression murderous. "Why, you haggardly old clapperdudgeon, I'll-"

The corporal's pole-arm swept across his comrade's path, clanging off the breastplate. "Hold, Stephen. He's harmless enough." He looked up at the carter with a wry chuckle. "Age loosens the tongue as sure as any strong drink." His eyes, small and keen, roved over the cart. "Empty. You're a gong farmer?"

The carter leaned to the side to peer into the bustling dockyard beyond. He could see long boathouses flanking a central thoroughfare, interspersed with rows of dwellings that were presumably built to house shipwrights, labourers, victuallers, officers and the many other tradesmen that would populate such a place. There were administration buildings, constructed in rich red brick, alongside busy workshops, brew-houses, storehouses and a multitude of other such places. It was a gigantic place, a town within a town and, with defences continually strengthened due to perpetual conflict with the Spanish and Dutch, it put him in mind of a small fortress.

He sniffed, offended. "Not any old gong. I've no interest in cowpats and dog turds. I am here at the behest of the venerable Doctor Phineas Welch. You've heard of him?"

The corporal shook his head. "I have not."

"Then it is a sore loss for you." The old man squinted at the peaked morions that protected the soldiers' skulls. "I cannot tell if you yet require Doctor Welch's services but time will surely compel you to seek him out."

"The fool speaks in riddles, Corporal," the taller guard, Stephen, said angrily, still smarting from the previous exchange. "Send him on his way!"

The carter shook his head. "Phineas Welch has made his name and fortune by coaxing the most lustrous locks from the most hirsute of pates."

"He cures baldness?" the corporal asked.

"Cures?" The carter tilted back his deeply lined face to guffaw at the sky. "Purges, banishes, expels!" He tapped the side of his nose conspiratorially, dropping his tone as if spies lurked on all sides. "But his secret ingredient is the dung of chickens. To be mixed with ash, oak bark, walnut leaves and the fat of a brown bear."

The corporal frowned. "A bear?"

"The fiercer the better! Now, you have poultry here, yes?"

The corporal shared a glance with Stephen and the pair instinctively looked back through the gateway and into the dockyard. "More than the sea breeze can contain."

Stephen cursed at a private memory. "If I had a penny for every time I'd fouled my boots in droppings, I'd be able to buy one of these ships."

"There you have it!" the carter exclaimed. "Divine providence at work! Praise be and hallelujah!" He winked, gathering up the reins with one gnarled hand and pointing into the dockyard with the other. "I have my wagon and my shovel. Sally forth, master soldier and let us relieve your besieged nostrils!"

*

Marek Novak could not wait to return to the high seas. He had rested well since arriving in England all those weeks ago. The blockade of Cadiz had hardly proved a great strain, for the Spanish treasure fleet Blake had intended to waylay had never arrived, the great galleons, pregnant with gold, sitting tight in the Americas, far beyond the Commonwealth's reach. Even so, that did not render shore leave unwelcome. After months of gales and rainfall, weevil infested victuals and grinding monotony, a spell upon terra firma had been just the tonic Marek's mind and body required. The exotic delights of the Southwark stews and the profits of pugilism only enhanced matters. Yet now, an hour before dusk, it was time to go home, to the creaking timbers and the roaring waves and a bed slung from rafters. A warship was the kind of place that a man like Marek could make his own. A little floating fiefdom, where the murky, dangerous world below decks offered opportunity for one willing to impress his captain and cut the throats of his rivals.

Yes, he thought, as he stepped out of The Bridge and buckled his sword belt, it was time to take to the sea once more. He imagined the ship *Diamond* waiting for them just over the horizon. "Come, my boys, let us make ourselves known to our brethren."

At his back came the rest of his company, most pressing calloused palms into eyes assailed by the fresh breeze and bright sunlight. A heavy night had come at the usual price and more than one man vomited on the cobbles. Marek was unconcerned with their collective stupor, so long as each man had legs enough to make it to the end of the dock and board the pinnace that had moored above the mouth of the Camber. He breathed deeply of the salt air, revelled in the caws of the gulls and resolved not to dwell on a former Parliamentarian cavalry officer who had stolen his most prized possession. The arrival of Maddocks had thrown him off kilter, admittedly, with claims that Lyle intended to bring the bible to its rightful owner but Marek's time had run out and so, therefore, had Botolph's. A pity but not something over which to lose sleep.

He looked round at the bleary gathering, finding one face in particular. "I salute your courage, young Botolph, for you walk to your death like a man."

The boy, wrists bound tightly at the small of his back, did not answer. On either side, Louis and Duncan, his perpetual gaolers, gave grim smiles. Their saturnine captive had grown a sparse layer of fluff upon his upper lip over the last few days, which made him look a fraction older, but it also provided stark contrast for his sickly sallow skin. He had suffered, it was true, so perhaps putting him out of his misery was, in some way, a kindness.

Marek sucked at his own whiskers, a veritable hedge in comparison to Botolph's. "There are worse ways to die than drowning, boy, believe me. Your wits would scatter if I described the things I have seen." He clapped his hands suddenly. "Let us be done and away, my friends. Bring him to the water's edge."

It was a matter of yards from the door of The Bridge to the end of Camber Dock, though they were forced to run a gauntlet of netting, discarded cordage and crab traps over the slick cobbles. Below them, bobbing in the teal waters of Portsmouth Haven, was a large pinnace, the boat dispatched from the *Diamond* to collect its hands. It dwarfed the only other moored vessel, a tiny skiff, with its rows of benches and banks of oars, the two boats putting Marek in mind of a whale and its calf. The majority of the pinnace's oarsmen were absent, having slipped over to The Point's central street, no doubt, to seek a pot of ale while the moment was opportune. One man had drawn the short straw, left behind to hail and board the passengers. He was laid out on one of the rowing benches, catching a surreptitious moment's sleep, watched only by a pair of beggars who were huddled beneath a painted mooring post at the edge of the quay. As he led the way to the pinnace, Marek barked in irritation at the slumbering sailor, expecting more pomp and circumstance for a man of his repute. Across the short stretch of water that formed the Camber's mouth, startled seagull chicks scattered en masse from the edges of the boats tied to the wooden jetty that served the main town. The birds screeched madly, their speckled brown bodies a blur against the grey sky.

"Alms, sir."

Marek slowed, looking down as he noticed a single arm, slender and bony, protrude from the filthy bundle of rags at the foot of the mooring post. Two pairs of eyes glinted up at him like jewels in a dung heap. The ripe stench of excrement drifted off the threadbare scraps in nauseating waves, making Marek put his sleeve across his mouth and nose. "Get away, you filthy crones."

The arm retracted but the beggar went on, "Alms for a poor, blind veteran."

Marek stopped just short of the reeking creatures. "Veteran of what?"

"Naseby Field," came a voice that was weak and cracking. "Worcester and many more."

"Very likely, I am sure," Marek scoffed.

"Veteran of a campaign in the Hampshire hills too," the beggar said, "at a place called Chalton. Perhaps you know it?"

Marek Nowak drew his sword. "You!"

But before he could lunge, the rags fell away like the scales over St Paul's eyes, to reveal a man and a young girl, both crouching, both holding pistols that were primed and cocked. The man's firearm consumed Marek's attention, for it was large and double-barrelled and it was trained directly on his stomach.

The Ironside Highwayman stood up. He gave a wry smile, even as Marek's men drew their own weapons. "Well, gentlemen. Here we all are once more."

Marek did not expect to see Lyle again and the surprise only now gave way to a smouldering rage. Through clenched teeth he said, "Let us hope *something* is different from our last meeting, *Skurwysyn*."

The beggar, Lyle, stooped briefly to pick up a cloth sack, hitherto obscured amongst the stinking rags at his feet. "You mean this?"

Marek watched the sack hang heavy in Lyle's grip, knowing immediately what lay within. "You have it," he said softly and the knowledge kindled new flames within his chest. "I knew it," he tried to say, though his voice had become a deep growl. He glanced over his shoulder to the men braced for violence. "Did I not say?" He was answered by a ripple of snarls and oaths and pledges of murder.

Lyle was standing straight now, gathered to his full height. "For what it's worth, it was stolen by a man named Whistler."

Marek spat derisively. "I care not for the web's threads, only for the spider."

Lyle shook his head. "Not one of my people. I merely found him for you." He gave a sardonic smile. "By rights, you owe me a bounty." He shook the sack. "You can have the pages and I'll take the cover."

Marek was positively alight with rage now. It took every ounce of strength to keep himself in check. After all, what good was his bible if it accompanied a bullet in the guts? "Return my property and I will return this streak of piss."

Lyle's green eyes drifted past Marek to take in the sight of

Botolph, bruised but whole, pinioned between Frenchman and Scotsman, just as he had been at Chalton. "What is so special about this book? It has a goodly amount of gold, I grant you but I'd wager a man such as you has plenty more treasure stowed away."

Marek stared at the sack that still gently swung like a pendulum from his enemy's hand. "That is Inca gold. It has…" he paused, groping in his mind for a word to do it justice, "power."

"Inca?" the little girl at Lyle's side chirped, astonishingly brightly for a child caught in a standoff.

"One of the tribes of the Americas," Lyle explained.

"Tribe?" Marek said contemptuously. "It was an empire. That gold was taken from the Ransom Room itself." He could hear his own voice thicken but was powerless to stop it. The provenance of the bible was what made it so special. "The very room where Atahualpa surrendered his kingdom to the conquistadors. After the battle of Cajamarca, Emperor Atahualpa offered Pizarro to buy his liberty by filling the room where he was kept prisoner with gold. That blood payment was melted down into ingots, divided amongst the conquering Spaniards and shipped home." He pointed the tip of his cutlass at Lyle. "Tell me. Have you heard of Batih?"

"The massacre?" replied Lyle.

Marek nodded. "I was there. After the battle, the Tartars of Crimea sold us like cattle to Ukrainian Cossacks, Satan devour them all."

"They executed many of your countrymen, I know."

"Many?" Marek echoed disdainfully, the choice of word utterly offensive to his ears. "There were five thousand of us, *Skurwysyn*. Hogtied and helpless. They disembowelled and beheaded us." He felt tears prick his eyes, hot and unstoppable. "It took them two whole days."

"But you survived."

"I worked the ropes loose. Hid under the corpses. When the Cossacks were gone, I crawled free." He twitched his wrist so that the cutlass slid down to point at the sack. "That book was in the hill of corpses. Right there with me. I do not know where it came from or who dropped it. But it found me. Saved me then and kept me alive since. That book is a potent thing. God's word and a blood curse, combined. It has kept me safe these many years, when, by rights, I should have perished a hundred times." He risked a quick glance back at Botolph. "I will return this whelp to you, upon my honour, if you hand me that sack."

Lyle seemed to wait for an age as he weighed a decision that was cruelly limited. Marek heard noise, the muffled voices of men calling to one another in the distance and recognised them as those of the *Diamond*'s oarsmen, returning to the pinnace for the journey out to Spithead. He could have laughed aloud. The highwayman had placed himself between Marek's dozen killers and the Camber's inky depths. A fool, if ever there was one. Lyle moved then and Marek felt his entire body zing with relief, for the Englishman had handed his pistol to the girl so that he might step forwards in unarmed parley, breaking the spell of the standoff. After three tentative paces, as if he approached a crazed colt, he lowered his hand to put the cloth sack on the ground. He kicked it, once, sending it tumbling over the cobbles to rest between the two parties. Then he retreated, as slow and measured as his advance had been. The first move had been made. Marek bowed. When he straightened, he twisted to jerk a chin at Duncan and Louis, who immediately shoved their captive away from the gathered men.

"You're free, boy," Marek said as Botolph, hands still bound, stumbled and lurched his way to the far side of the quay. Lyle's accomplice, the little wench, took hold of the bewildered boy and guided him by an arm to the small skiff that rose and fell gently in the shadow of the pinnace. Marek caught Botolph's eye as the lad made an ungainly descent of the dock's sandy slope. He read confusion there and well he might, for the Pole had promised a death this day. But it was not Botolph's death Marek so desperately sought. He raised his cutlass and went to the slaughter.

Lyle knew that Marek would attack and he knew that the sailor would be fast but still he was unprepared. The cutlass lanced forth as its bearer skipped half a dozen staccato steps in what seemed like the blink of an eye. Lyle only just managed to slide his own blade from its scabbard in time to bring it up for the parry and his twisting, grunting retreat was met with a thunderous cheer from the watching crowd, a couple of whom made to lend their leader a hand.

"Hold!" Marek snarled, spittle flecking his whiskers. He stood poised for the next attack, sword high like a battle standard. His face was reddening rapidly and he breathed hard but bloodlust made him dangerous and Lyle stayed back. "Any man interferes, I'll run him through myself!"

The mariners stood firm. The duellists were ten yards apart now. Lyle pushed forwards his left foot and turned his shoulders, presenting the narrowest target possible behind the ornate Pappenheimer rapier in his left hand. He edged in, getting the measure of his opponent and the blades touched at the tips, their metallic song ringing across the water.

Marek's eyes tightened and he sucked in a quick breath. Lyle read it and danced backwards as the Pole lunged, wildly and with a great roar that had the gulls scattering and the sailors bellowing their support. Lyle swept the cutlass aside; once, twice, thrice. Each blow sending spears of pain through his half-healed bullet wound. He bit down on the inside of his mouth as if he could distract himself and jabbed his own blade up at the bigger man's throat, feeling Marek bat it away with his iron guard. Then Lyle went low, for the groin and Marek managed to twirl aside, saving himself by a fraction.

They set themselves again. Lungs heaving in time. Marek growled, "You thought your actions-would go unavenged, *Skurwysyn*? You think me a man to be deceived? To be made a laughing-stock?"

"I did not steal the book," Lyle said, though he knew his protests were futile. "Botolph did not steal the book."

Marek spat. "I will cut you for every lie to roll off your forked tongue." He laughed maniacally, drunk on bloodlust and violence. "Then I will cut off your tongue too!"

They came together. Marek slashed in huge arcs that might have felled trees, trying to take Lyle's head clean from his shoulders. The highwayman, surprised by the brawny sailor's agility, scrambled backwards, swaying out of range, then spun like an acrobat, countering the assault with a flurry of his own blows that had Marek recoiling haphazardly.

The sailors brayed as though betting on a dog fight. Lyle grimaced at the burning pain in his shoulder-blade. Marek stooped slightly, bracing one hand on a thigh, chest heaving in and out.

"Enough?" Lyle said. "Take ship, sirrah. Let us leave here with the boy, with no more harm done."

Marek pounced. Baring his teeth like a crazed animal, he screamed a war cry in his native tongue and swung the curved cutlass in two hands, a Viking berserker at a shield wall. Lyle parried the first sweeping cut but lambent flares of agony licked at the tender flesh at his left shoulder and he could not mount a riposte, reeling away instead.

Visibly short of breath, Marek slowed, swashing the cutlass in front like a scythe as he kept his furious glare fixed on Lyle. "You'll die, *Skurwysyn,*" he sneered. "Your corpse will feed the fish."

If Colonel Francis Maddocks could have reached Portsmouth Point at a gallop, he would have but Point Gate was narrow and, at the zenith of a short winter's day, heavy with traffic. It was a bottleneck of the most infuriating kind and it took several minutes of berating by the colonel and his officers, all standing in stirrups and waving pistols, to get the carts, animals and pedestrians moving. The fact that the congestion had been exacerbated by his own meticulous searches was not lost on him.

The point, though, was moot. For a message direct from The Bridge tavern had reached him at his roadblock. The place was a bawdy house as well as a tavern, its patrons savouring a good deal more than local ale and, though Maddocks was technically obliged to close such an establishment down, he had taken the opportunity to place the lewd women in his pay, just in case Lyle managed the impossible. Now, according to one of the resident slatterns, the impossible had happened. Somehow the infernal highwayman and his gang had inveigled their way onto The Point. Well, thought Maddocks as his troopers clattered through the gates, the elusive and arrogant brigand had finally come unstuck. He kicked his mount so that it brought up the rear of the riders as they funnelled into single file behind their flapping colour. "They're rats in a barrel, my lads!" he called exultantly. "Rats in a barrel!"

They managed the hint of a canter as they moved north along Broad Street, the central artery along which The Point's life teemed. Maddocks urged his horse to extra speed as he gradually made his way to the front of the line, bellowing at folk too stupid or too lazy to move out of his way and nearly trampling a youngster who was not paying attention as he pushed a barrow of wizened apples across the road. It was only a matter of half a mile, taking a right onto East Street and then straight onto the quay but it was a maddeningly sluggish business nonetheless and he feared he would be too late, that his men would thunder onto Camber Dock only to discover Marek reunited with his precious bible and Lyle vanished back into the town.

It was with pleasure, then, that he caught sight of the duel that was playing out on the slick cobbles between the dock and The Bridge tavern. Samson Lyle and Marek Nowak, soldier against sailor, rapier against cutlass. Maddocks could only see the confrontation because of the saddle's high vantage, for the patch of land given over to the snarling contest was entirely shielded by the bodies of bellowing, jeering men he recognised to be the members of Marek's gun crew. Which gave him pause. He had imagined joining the fray. Surrounding Lyle and lending the might of his beloved harquebusiers to the chase. But to do that he would have to first make a path through the sailors.

"Clear them, sir?" Captain Beck said, reading his thoughts as he reined in at his side.

Maddocks shook his head. "Why bother? Lyle is trapped. Nowak has apparently decided not to make the exchange in a gentlemanly manner." He took a drink from the flask in his saddlebag while he watched the fight unfold. "Send a squad back to Point Gate, Captain. A matter of precaution."

"By the looks of things," Beck said, "Lyle is taking a hiding. I had heard he was a master."

Maddocks nodded. "Was." He swigged again. As he did so his eyes slid across the tiny bay to the row of fishing boats moored beside the Oyster Street jetty. There were just two figures on the timber walkway, presumably attracted by the noise of clashing steel as it drifted across the water. "Pity there aren't more witnesses to this most joyous occasion, eh?" He arched his back, cracking it and yawned. "No, Captain. The playhouses may have been suppressed but entertainments can yet be found. Let Nowak make an end of the Ironside Highwayman and we shall cheer his every strike."

Lyle's left shoulder blade burned like the fires of damnation. He gave ground again and again, wheeling about when space was short, offering painful ripostes to buy time and push Marek briefly onto the back foot. But he was losing. He was the superior swordsman, they both knew it but Marek's unrelenting attacks, fuelled by his bullish size and terrible rage, simply battered his smaller opponent, the clash of steel deafening as he smashed his way into – and through – Lyle's defensive postures. Closing on him, devouring the open-air Lyle so carefully maintained between them.

Marek, his heavy, rasping breaths audible above the shouts of his comrades, girded himself for a wild lunge. Lyle bit down on his bottom lip to distract from the pain and leapt backwards to receive the frenzied onslaught. The blades collided high, slid down the length of the killing edge and hilts clanged so that the pair came together in a strange embrace of snarls and grimaces. Lyle did all he could, lent his whole strength to the wrestle but he felt himself wilt beneath Marek's irresistible power. He jumped away, jabbing the rapier at Marek's windpipe to force the Pole into a desperate parry that would temporarily staunch the tide of his attack.

"You have been tricked, *Skurwysyn*!" Marek snarled, grinning and he danced on tiptoes for a moment, demonstrating an evident reserve of stamina and belying a face of livid crimson. "I am a pugilist. A good one. I do not tire!"

Lyle braced again. Marek had his back to the dock and Lyle leaned to the side to look past him at the waiting pinnace. The boatman was standing on the rowing bench. To Lyle's unqualified relief, the man raised a hand and waved.

Colonel Francis Maddocks did not even bother to affect the dour dignity demanded by his rank. He grinned as he chewed cardamom seeds and witnessed the demolition of his nemesis. It would have been more satisfying – downright poetic, even – if it had been Maddocks' own sword that made the final cut but greed and pride were both sins. He would have to make do with the memories.

And the end was close. Jesus but it was achingly close. Lyle had crumpled, forced into desperate evasion that could not last when pursued with such venomous alacrity. He found himself recalling that moment before Christmas, when he had pulled his pistol's trigger in the woods below Butser Hill. It had not been a killing shot, the range too great but the ball had found its mark nonetheless. Had punched into Lyle's upper back to make him sway and lurch and cling onto his mount's neck for all he was worth.

"Not all blows are immediately fatal," Maddocks muttered.

"Sir?"

Maddocks glanced to his side. "No matter, Captain Beck." As his gaze returned to the crowd and the duel, he noticed once more the figures on the timber jetty. He might have paid them no heed, except that they had moved to the middle of the long platform that stretched into the Camber from the town wharves. Idly, he watched them. They were kneeling together, huddled beneath their hoods like a pair of incanting witches. Then he saw the glow. Dim and orange, even gentle. Not a flame, as such but an ember.

"Slow match," he said to himself.

Beck, enthralled by the fight, answered distractedly, "Match, sir?"

"Jesu. They have slow matches over there. Look. See it?" A low, whispering dread came over Maddocks then. A knot started to form, deep within his core. "Wait. Something isn't right."

Lyle gave up his fencer's stance and stood flat-footed, lowering the Pappenheimer as if to concede the day.

"Come, *Skurwysyn*!" Marek roared, his nostrils flaring, eyes wide like twin moons. He tilted back his head and laughed; a sound that was wild and visceral. "And I thought you were a master! Let us finish this!"

Marek had his back to the water, blocking Lyle's view of the boats but he glimpsed the man in the pinnace as he jumped nimbly from the warship's vessel over to Bella's boat. "I was shot in my left shoulder," he called, loud enough for the baying mob to hear. "The wound has not yet fully healed. Saps my strength something grievous." He shifted his hips and torso, resuming the fighter's stance but this time it was his right foot that slid forwards. "Fortunately," he went on, swapping the rapier into his other palm. "I am not left-handed."

Marek's jaw dropped open. He stood there, dumbstruck and confused, as his chest heaved, his face a scarlet mask. The other sailors, deafened by their own shouts and blinded by shared bloodlust, simply called him on, charging their leader with finishing the job.

Indignation lit up Marek's eyes then. Lyle could see that the revelation would not smother the fire in Marek's belly but add fuel to it and he inched back voluntarily, letting the bigger man come on.

And Marek charged.

He raised the cutlass high and bolted like a demented ox, oaths tumbling from his mouth as he roared. Lyle bent at the knees, placed his aching left arm safely at his back and gauged the distance. He transferred his weight onto the front foot as Marek loomed above him, flicked out his blade to receive the blow, then pirouetted like a dancer. Steel met steel, Marek's huge power absorbed by a rejuvenated Lyle and the highwayman deflected the cutlass, sending it wide as his body ghosted under Marek's right arm. He completed the turn as Marek blundered past and lashed out with the flat of his sword, striking the Pole across his rump.

Marek brayed like a mule. Overreaching himself and unable to reel in his lunge, he was thrown off balance and he stumbled forth like a toppling building to smash, face first, onto the cobbles in a tangle of limbs, his cutlass skittering and clattering away.

The crowd fell silent, every man stunned into dumb inertia.

Every man except one. Samson Lyle did not linger or gloat. He ran for the edge of the dock, not breaking his stride as he stooped to scoop up the cloth sack and bounded straight down onto the sandy slope. He leapt for all he was worth, sailing over the sloshing shallows and crashing, pell-mell, into the little boat that Bella had managed to extricate from its mooring rope. It lurched under his weight, water slapping the sides and spilling over to shower the hull.

"Could have stabbed us with that," Eustace Grumm said, still breathing hard from his exertions over on the pinnace.

"My apologies," Lyle answered, grinning at Bella as he sheathed the Pappenheimer. He dropped the sack in the bottom of the boat, gathering up the oars and hauling hard, pulling against the tangled weeds with their fat bubbles. His shoulder wound made it a struggle and Grumm gathered up the second pair, swearing viciously as he bent himself to the effort. Between them on the middle bench, Botolph shivered. Bella wrapped her beggar's rags about his shoulders. The thud and slap of the oars played a rhythm under the growing chorus of incensed shouts coming from the quay. But they were building momentum now, edging away from The Point and into the expanse of the harbour with every oar stroke. The dark water, flecked with bits of pale crab and green weed, sluiced about the hull in time with the boat's motion, shifting the bible in its cloth sack like flotsam on the tide.

Up on Camber Dock, the crowd surged. They were a matter of yards away and Lyle twisted to look into their grimacing faces. They spat curses and threats, jabbed the air with swords and several were kneeling to load firearms. Lyle caught sight of Marek. The huge gun captain, beside the mooring post, was unflinching, impassive, though his gaze contained a wrath that almost made Lyle quell. Almost.

He inclined his head, acknowledging their duel. Marek's eye twitched at the corner and he said something, though Lyle could not hear it and then the sailors were cascading down the slope to the pinnace.

"They're coming," Botolph said. His voice was weak, a mere husk but there was vigour in his trembling hands and raw intensity in his gaze. He was staring in abject terror at the pinnace. "They're c… c… coming."

Lyle leaned forwards and patted Botolph's shoulder. "No, young sir, they are not."

Behind him, just as the first of Marek's howling pack reached the water's edge, the pinnace exploded.

Maddocks' horse was turning circles as he bellowed, whirling his sword above his head to provide a focal point in the commotion. "On me! On me!"

The harquebusiers, many having dismounted during the duel, scurried like mice to their positions, leaping up into saddles without even bothering to cram helmets over their heads or fasten gauntlets to their arms. Many were utterly bemused by the sudden turmoil, for they were spread thinly across the lawless spur of land, manning checkpoints at major taverns and street junctions all the way back to Point Gate and had no idea of what had unfolded. But they all heard the explosion.

The horsemen gathered en mass, churning about their leader like an iron-clad eddy, eyes darting back and forth between colonel and quayside.

When enough of his troopers had coalesced, Maddocks gauged the situation. His first thought was to storm the dock but the sailors had recoiled from the slope amid a shower of water and splinters. They congregated now about the mooring post, impotent in their rage, still screaming obscenities into the harbour as a thick pall of white smoke roiled about them like acrid fog. If they were a hindrance before, they were downright impassable now and he knew the chance to ride Lyle down had gone. He wrenched savagely on the reins, levelling the long, single-edged blade in a south-easterly direction. "To the town, damn your eyes! The town! Make for the jetty!"

Lyle and Grumm rowed hard. Marek and his men were stranded on Portsmouth Point but that did not mean the fugitives were home and dry. They could not rest until they had cleared the harbour and its formidable gun batteries. Still, though, Lyle felt a tide of relief swell in his chest and dampen the pain in his shoulder.

"What was that?" Botolph Spendlove said. His eyes, red-rimmed and glazed, were fixed on the entrance to the Camber, where a warship's large boat had erupted in a column of flame and timber and froth and now, as shards rained down to dapple the surface of the water, the pinnace had already lost its stern to the chill depths, the bow sitting high, right out of the water, as if lifted by some invisible sea creature. "Cannon? Mortar?" Now he turned, becoming frantic as he looked to the blockhouse on the Gosport side of the harbour. "Do they bombard us from the fort?"

"A petard," Grumm answered, proffering the puzzled young man with a decayed grin. "One of God's most sublime creations."

"There's nought of God in it," Lyle admonished the Cornishman. "A rudimentary device," he said to Botolph. "Highly dangerous, which is why," he winked, "it is crucial to have it set by an eminently expendable personage."

Grumm snorted but chose not to take the bait. "You takes a bell, cast in iron or brass. Fill it with black powder and fix it to a wooden base. Or, in this case, simply prop it in the floor of a wooden boat. Light the fuse and," he briefly released the oars so that he could clap his hands together, "boom."

"Evil contraptions," said Lyle. "Had occasion to employ them during the wars." He slid his backside round to take sight of the dock. The sailors were still there but the pinnace had all but gone. His gaze drifted to the left, to the jetty that extended from the Oyster Street wharf and the small fleet of fishing boats moored on both sides, noses inwards, like so many piglets at a sow. From the town came a sudden, deep thrum of hoof-beats and out from one of the alleys streamed horsemen. Dozens of them. They galloped in pairs, wrapped in leather and metal, barred visors pulled over most of their faces, a saffron-coloured cornet fluttering in the van. The small flag bore the head of a black lion.

The cavalrymen began to shout threats, just as the sailors had done but they were quickly silenced by the barks of officers. Then they were dismounting, gathering about one man in particular and Lyle saw that it was Francis Maddocks himself.

All eyes in the skiff had gone to the jetty now. "He found us, then," Bella muttered, her attempt to keep her tone light undermined by an unmistakable tension.

"Now, your petard," Lyle went on as they watched the troopers file onto the timber walkway, evidently intent on commandeering the fishing fleet. "One might secure it to a gate using hooks, or prop it against a bridge with beams."

"They're going to catch us," Botolph whispered.

"The shape of the thing," Lyle went on, undeterred, "concentrates the explosive so it may be targeted. In this case," he jerked back his head to indicate the sunken pinnace, "it was discharged downwards. In that case, however," he said, levering up an oar to point it at the jetty, "you will note the blast goes up."

Botolph frowned, opening his mouth to speak but the words were drowned out by a deluge of concussive noise as the second petard ignited, ripping through the end of the jetty from one of the footings beneath. The soldiers recoiled as one, scrambling away as the water and the sky seethed and kindling tumbled through a new bank of sulphurous cloud to scatter Oyster Street, The Point and the modest bay in between.

Then all was silent. Marek and his crew stood, mutely now, on Camber Dock, while Maddocks and his harquebusiers milled before the jagged remains of the jetty, their senses scrambled by the huge explosion, their plans in disarray. Just below them, tantalisingly out of reach, the empty fishing boats gently drifted loose to bob into open water.

Lyle let go of his oars. He reached out to pat Botolph's shoulder. "You're safe now, lad. Let's get you home." Then he stood up, taking a fistful of the soaking cloth sack. The skiff pitched alarmingly as he turned but he managed to pull the golden bible free, the pages within utterly ruined. Mercifully, that mattered to Lyle not a bit. He held it aloft, for Marek and Maddocks to see and offered a deep, lingering bow.

*

Near Alverstoke, Hampshire

The skiff slid onto the pebble beach with a hiss. Lyle jumped, boots splashing and crunching at once and dragged the vessel a few more yards so that it was safely grounded. It was dark but the sky was clear and the moon iridescent. He scanned the ridge at the top of the beach. It was empty, save for a line of grass tufts that curved before the salty breeze.

"Come," he said. "We'll find the road beyond that low dune."

They abandoned the boat, pushing it back into the sea so that, wherever it finally washed up, it would not give a clue to their whereabouts. Then they trudged up the beach, the gushing surf at their backs, tired bodies stumbling over the ever-shifting shingle.

Botolph was first to speak. The miseries of his captivity and the shocking nature of his rescue had seemed to tip him over some imperceptible ledge, so that he had withdrawn into himself as they fought the Solent's pernicious currents. He had hunkered into his blankets as dusk had crept in, his eyes staring vacantly at the shore and battened down any words that might have come. It was a revelation for the others, then, when his pale face shone with sudden animation at the ridge's summit.

"Papa!" he exclaimed, shedding the makeshift shawl so that it was snatched by the wind to tumble back down the beach. "Papa, I am here!"

The north face of the ridge was a gentle slope that began as stony sand and finished as grass, joining a narrow trackway that plunged into rolling pasture. There was little sign of civilisation in any direction, save for the vertical lines of smudged stars, about a mile to the northeast, that spoke of a village's thin smoke trails. All around them the landscape was empty, except for the lone wagon, down on the trackway, that was hitched to a pair of strong looking horses. Seated above them on the wagon's bench were two figures. Their faces were too far off to identify but one had a head of silver hair and the other wore a simple white cap.

Botolph was already running when the people in the wagon clambered down. Arms aloft, he dashed over the sand, sliding and leaping by turns until he hit the firmer grass and all the while he called for the father he thought never again to see.

The Spendloves embraced. The three of them, down beside the waiting horses, locking arms and weeping as one, voices muffled as temples pressed. Lyle, Grumm and Bella grinned and laughed as they strode to meet a family reunited.

It was Amelia who broke away first, coming to stand before Lyle, the highwayman gingerly rolling his damaged shoulder. She reached out, touching his elbow. His eyes fell unbidden to her hand.

"How do you fare?" she asked, squeezing his arm gently.

"Hurts," he said, self-consciousness making him brusque. He forced himself to look up, softening his tone. "I shall be hearty enough before long. Bullet wounds are generally not hospitable to fighting duels or rowing the Solent."

She smiled at that. The ochre flecks in her brown eyes shimmering like quicksilver in the moonlight. "Everything you have done, Major Lyle," she shook her head in wonder, "we can scarcely fathom, let alone repay."

Lyle placed his hand across hers. Her skin was warm despite the chill in the night air. "Be glad you have your brother back. It is enough."

They parted as her father approached, Lyle grudgingly letting her fingers slip away. Before he could react, Spendlove thrust out his arms and enveloped him in a tight embrace, sobbing through his joy.

"You must thank your friend, Samson," Spendlove said when they parted. "Dear Tom risked so much."

Lyle produced the golden bible from within his coat. "He and the other fishermen will have this. Payment, in lieu of their jetty and fleet, most of which is now scattered about the harbour, I'd wager."

"Did you ever intend to return it to Marek?" Botolph said, coming to stand beside his father.

"Certainly," Lyle replied. "I changed my mind when he tried to run me through." He was gratified to see Botolph's mouth twitched at the corners. It was the first time he had seen the lad smile.

"Pious men are wont to do foolish things," Spendlove said sagely.

"Not piety," said Lyle. "It was not the scriptures he revered but the gold itself. Inca gold. He believed it offered him protection. A talisman." He glanced down at the book. "Now it can be another's talisman. Tom can melt it down and buy new nets."

Spendlove laughed. "A whole new fleet!"

"They lit the fuse," Botolph said to Lyle, his voice querulous with evident astonishment. "My father and sister. Did you know? Out on the jetty!"

Lyle slapped him on the back. "I am aware of that."

"It was the major's idea," Amelia chided her brother, punching his shoulder playfully.

"Secured," their father said, "in ominously professional fashion by Mister Grumm, here."

"Those petards," Botolph addressed Grumm now. "How did you come by them?"

"Made them with mine own fair hands, boy," Grumm said with a roguish cackle.

"He stole them," said Bella.

Grumm held up his hands as if surrendering to some unseen force. "Stole is a strong word."

She snorted. "It's the right word, you sly old stoat."

He screwed up his craggy face. "The bottles and the fuses I stole." He leaned in to Botolph's ear, whispering, "Inveigled my way into the navy dockyard, didn't I, lad?" He laughed when the young man's mouth flapped in amazement. "Dressed myself up as a gong collector, of all things!"

"You are a marvel, sir," Botolph said, his tone hushed with awe.

"That I am and you can be sure to remind the major, here, eh?"

"What of the other ingredients?" Wardley Spendlove asked.

"Half the black powder was purchased with the major's funds," Grumm said.

Spendlove shook his head at the audacity of it. "You bribed a dockyard worker?"

"Indeed. The other half came from a crate of grenadoes, which were gifted to me, on account of this blade," he patted his waist as he spoke, "and its proximity to the storeman's stones. Then I loaded up my cart, buried the lot under a pile o' chicken dung and off I went."

"I thank you, sir," Botolph said.

Spendlove gathered his son and daughter in his arms. "We all thank you."

Grumm waved them away, suddenly embarrassed. "Never a doubt nor hesitation."

Lyle smiled, deciding not to mention Grumm's early views on the matter. Instead he looked over at the wagon that would be their transport for the next couple of hours. They would travel together initially as they departed the Gosport peninsula, seeking tracks with the deepest hedgerows and always scrutinising the horizon for horsemen. But they had rowed west out of Portsmouth, agreeing to rendezvous here, thus placing the entire harbour between them and their pursuers. Maddocks would be forced to ride the full fifteen miles around the water, with no clue as to where his quarry would alight. When the sun finally made inroads, the two groups would have parted, the Spendloves taking the highroad to the west while Lyle's gang would plunge into the vast countryside to the east, keeping to the sunken, shadowy lanes that criss-crossed field and forest. He said to his old school master, "Wales for you?"

Spendlove nodded. "I have kin in Pembrokeshire. Seems a good moment to pay them a visit."

"You have money?"

"Enough to see us there safely." He gathered his children close, one in each arm. "And you?"

An intense feeling of longing smouldered like a brazier in Lyle's chest as he watched Spendlove's hand slide about Amelia's shoulders. He cleared his throat, suddenly ashamed. "Retrieve the horses," he said thickly, "and wend our way back."

"They'll hunt you," Amelia said.

"I wouldn't have it any other way." Lyle disguised the lie with a broad grin. He turned to Bella and Grumm. "Ready? Then let's go home."

Historical Note

The Rule of the Major-Generals was a 15-month period of direct military government during Oliver Cromwell's Protectorate. The new system was commissioned in October 1655 and the country divided into 12 regions, each governed by a Major-General who was answerable only to the Lord Protector.

The first duty of the Major-Generals was to maintain security by suppressing unlawful assemblies, disarming Royalists and apprehending thieves, robbers and highwaymen. To assist them in this work, they were authorised to raise their own militias.

Colonel Maddocks and his men are figments of my imagination, but William Goffe was indeed Major-General for Berkshire, Sussex and Hampshire, and it would have been his responsibility to hunt down Samson Lyle and men like him. Sadly, Lyle himself is a fictional character, but he is indicative of many outlaws of the period. Contrary to the classic tradition of the 18th Century dandy highwayman, mounted bandits have infested England's major roads for hundreds of years. Indeed, in 1572 Thomas Wilson wrote a dialogue in which one character commented that in England, highway robbers were likely to be admired for their courage, while another suggested that a penchant for robbery was one of the Englishman's besetting sins.

During the years immediately following the Civil Wars, highway banditry became more widespread simply due to the sheer number of dispossessed, heavily armed and vengeful former Royalists on the roads. This idea was the inspiration behind the Ironside Highwayman, though I felt it might be more interesting if my protagonist had been a Roundhead rather than a Cavalier.

The locations in the story are all real. The Red Lion at Chalton and The Court House at East Meon still stand today, while the gatehouse tower is all that's left of Warblington Castle. The site of Grange Farm in Petersfield has, in the intervening years, been home to a gas works, an abattoir and, latterly, a supermarket, but the impressive stone barn and coach house remains, and is now home to a GP surgery.

Portsmouth Point, or 'Spice Island' as it was (and is) often known, really was outside of the city boundary, separated by walls and a gate. It gained quite a reputation for lawlessness, vice and villain. The ideal place for a group of sailors to pass the time before joining ship! Incidentally, the Portsmouth Point name was commonly contracted to **Po'm. P.** when recorded in ships' logbooks to , giving rise to the nickname of "*Pompey*".

The Saxon church at Idsworth (Lyle would have known it as St Peter's, though it was later rededicated to St Hubert) is a gem, and highly evocative. Built by Earl Godwin (King Harold's father), it stood at the heart of a village that was ultimately abandoned during the Black Death. Now it stands alone and isolated, looking rather incongruous amongst the sweeping hills, but its interior bears the marks of the thriving community it once serviced. During Victorian renovation work, a range of beautiful 14th Century murals were discovered beneath layers of paint that had presumably been applied during the Reformation. Well worth a look if you're visiting the South Downs National Park.

Also by Michael Arnold

The Civil War Chronicles
Stryker and the Angels of Death (Novella)
Traitor's Blood
Devil's Charge
Hunter's Rage
Assassin's Reign
Warlord's Gold
The Prince's Gambit (Novella)
Marston Moor

The Highwayman Series
Highwayman: Ironside
Highwayman: Winter Swarm

The Joshua Hawke Thrillers
Corpse Thief

About the Author

Michael Arnold's interest in British history is lifelong, and childhood holidays were spent visiting castles and battlefields. He became a Sharpe junkie at the age of 13, and his particular fascination with the seventeenth century was piqued partly by the fact that his hometown, Petersfield, is steeped in the history of the period. Michael is the critically acclaimed author of The Civil War Chronicles, featuring the indomitable Captain Stryker, and is also the creator of the Corpse Thief series, in which he turns his attention to the dark underworld of Regency London's resurrectionists.

You can find out more about Michael by visiting the following places:

www.michael-arnold.net
Facebook: MichaelArnoldBooks
Twitter: @MikeArnold01
Instagram: michaelarnoldauthor

*

Printed in Great Britain
by Amazon

13256169R00091